SALVATION

Amelia Doss Series Book 3

ANDRE GONZALEZ
AUDREY BRICE

✿   I   ✿

Fifteen years after surviving a second near-death experience at the hands of Amelia Doss, Tyler Reynolds flailed around his bedroom, hopping around while he tried to slip into his dress pants as he finished getting ready for the day.

"Hey, babe," he whispered to his wife, Avery, still under the sheets. She didn't have to be up for another hour to get the kids ready and drop them off at daycare. "Have you seen my wallet? I can't remember where I put it last night when we got back from the ice cream shop."

Avery groaned, her blond hair splattered across the pillow as she rolled onto her side. "Kitchen counter," she mumbled.

"Okay, thanks. I love you." Tyler shuffled to the bed and planted a kiss on her forehead, moving through the dark room, the sun awaiting its ascent in the next half hour. Avery didn't flinch and returned to her light snooze as soon as Tyler stepped outside.

He finished dressing and ran a comb through his hair to tidy his appearance. Getting dressed in the dark had initially been a struggle, but he'd learned to adjust, laying his clothes out the night before, and using his cell phone's flashlight to grab things like his wallet and jewelry off his nightstand.

Tyler made his way down their upstairs hallway to check on the kids at the other end. He poked his head into his son's room first, and spotted the six-year-old out cold—the blankets a tangled mess, his arms splayed over the edge of the bed. The boy's name, Wyatt, decorated the wall above the bed in glow-in-the-dark letters. "Have a good day, little man," Tyler whispered, closing the door and crossing the hall where his three-year-old daughter, Charlotte, lay sound asleep, her body upside-down on the bed as her feet rested on the pillow.

Charlotte had the west-facing bedroom, something that made Tyler plenty jealous as it would remain nearly blacked out even after the sun had risen. But they needed to reserve it for Charlotte, or else she would be the first one awake, which meant everyone else would be shortly after.

"Have a good day, sweet girl," Tyler whispered, closing the door and taking soft steps down the stairwell that led to the main level.

Tyler and Avery had met during their junior year of college at a movie night hosted on campus. They had each gone to the event separately, with their own friends, and ended up sitting next to each other in the crowded courtyard during a showing of *A Nightmare on Elm Street*. Tyler had seen the movie at least two dozen times, and couldn't help but drop random factoids to Avery, who was sitting next to him. She had admitted to seeing it plenty of times, too, and their conversation eventually overpowered their desire to watch the movie. Afterward, they strolled downtown to grab late-night pizza and keep the discussion going.

All of that led to them getting married and moving back to Tyler's hometown of Ridgeway, where a new home development had gone up shortly after they graduated. The Mountain Vista Estates provided luxury-style homes for a reasonable budget, considering Ridgeway was still very much a small town despite its gradual growth.

Tyler taught U.S. History at his alma mater, Ridgeway High School, and Avery worked remotely as an architect for a firm with projects all around the world. They had looked at their finances and decided Tyler wouldn't even need to work if they lived in Ridgeway, but he didn't have any clue what he might do with so much free time. He had earned his degree in history, which had little use outside of teaching the subject to other students, or nosing around the archives at the public library.

Avery had the flexibility of being able to get the kids ready and dropped off at kindergarten and preschool. Tyler had to be at the high school by seven o'clock to prepare for the day ahead.

He rummaged through the kitchen cupboards, sure to first grab his wallet off the counter, and found a Pop-Tart for a quick breakfast. He missed having a full breakfast, but tried to keep the clattering of dishes to a minimum while everyone else slept.

The mornings were lonely, but they made up for it on the weekends when Avery cooked pancakes every Saturday. The family dog, Buster, dragged himself from his bed in the living room and whimpered at Tyler's feet.

"Stop begging," he gently chided the young dachshund, and opened the back door to let the dog outside to relieve himself.

The cool morning air got sucked into the house, always brisk no matter the season. Tyler stuffed the rest of the Pop-Tart into his mouth before heading for the garage door and slipping into a jacket.

He had yet to shake the grogginess from his head, having stayed up late the night before reading Danny's newest novel. His best friend had struck success out of college, landing a publishing deal and eventually a couple of movie adaptations. Danny had become a popular horror novelist after a college professor suggested he try writing books instead of screenplays.

Danny Espinoza kept a property in Ridgeway, but split his time all around the country, and sometimes other countries, if he had an international book tour. They grabbed dinner when Danny was in town, which had become more frequent lately. Their conversations always drifted toward their disturbing memories of Amelia Doss, the topic impossible to avoid when they were in their hometown.

Tyler had pushed her from his thoughts for the most part, but working in the school where she had once slaughtered his teacher many years ago, his thoughts occasionally drifted into the darkness of remembering her kidnapping his mother, and nearly murdering him during a sexual encounter she had tricked him into back at Denver State University.

He shook his head free of the thoughts, picking up his briefcase and stepping into the garage. The door groaned as it slid open, the faintest splash of the morning's first crack of sunlight spilling across Tyler's Subaru sedan. He hopped in the car and pulled out of the neighborhood to make his daily journey across town.

His commute was typically when Amelia tried to pop back into his thoughts. He passed the convenience store where Amelia had murdered the owner when Tyler was in high school. He also passed the ditch where they had eventually found Bryson's body. It was impossible for Tyler to not think back to these prominent events in his life when driving by, and he always remembered when he and Danny had burned Bryson's letterman jacket that had suspiciously arrived at his college dorm room. Danny had insisted they do it, unsure if Amelia had potentially put a curse on the jacket, or if some part of her soul remained tethered to it.

They had driven up to the mountains for a weekend camping trip and tossed the jacket in the campfire, both breaking into an intense crying session, as it felt like they were once again saying goodbye to their friend.

The tickle of gooseflesh crept up his spine as he passed the ditch, and he couldn't help but wonder what Bryson might have made of his life had it not ended so tragically. He imagined Bryson would have earned an athletic scholarship and gone to any college of his choosing. Had his growth as an athlete continued on the track it was already on, he just might have gone professional. Bryson had always been ambitious, so even if a career in sports hadn't panned out, he surely would have landed a great job and started his perfect American family.

"Rest easy, my friend," Tyler said once he passed the ditch. He crossed the intersection where a left turn would have taken him to his parents' house. They usually met up for a meal once every weekend. Tyler's parents had both retired and enjoyed spending their time at the golf course or the new pool and hot tub they had installed in their backyard. The kids loved going over for a swim, so they often ended up there during the summers.

Tyler arrived at the school parking lot and pulled into his usual spot near the front entrance. Not all teachers arrived an hour before the morning bell, but a good amount did, Tyler spotting seven other vehicles this morning.

The football team's bus had been decorated with well-wishes and balloons as they were set to begin their season this upcoming Friday night. Despite the growth of Ridgeway, the residents still retained their obsession with the high school football team like any small town. Tyler had petitioned to have the football field named after Bryson, and the school had agreed to it. Bryson's jersey, with the number seven embroidered on it, hung in the broadcast booth perched atop the grandstands. Tyler would sometimes spend his lunch break in the booth just to be around the jersey and reminisce on the many times Bryson had led the team to victory. Friday nights in high school had formed some of his fondest memories, and he never wanted to let those go.

Tyler stepped out of his car and drew in a deep breath of the fresh mountain air. He had several doubts about moving back home after getting married, but was glad he had seen the decision through. No amount of distance from Ridgeway would erase the lingering horror that swam in his thoughts. Hell, Amelia had tracked him down in college when both he and Danny had ruled that as impossible. While there were good days and bad days, Tyler could always return home to his family for comfort. When he needed his nostalgia fulfilled, he could simply roam down the hallways of Ridgeway High, or go for a walk down Main Street and visit the restaurants he had frequented as a teenager.

Long gone were the days of rushing home after school to play video games and tear through a stack of homework. Evenings now consisted of baths for the kids, dinner, and a new stack of homework—one which he had to grade.

"Another day in paradise," he said as he approached the school. Tyler enjoyed his work, finding it a challenge to connect with teenagers daily, and even more challenging to connect the historical content he was teaching to modern times.

A sign hung over the main entrance that welcomed guests to Ridgeway High School, with a motivational quote along the bottom that read: *Are you giving your all today?*

Tyler slapped the sign as he entered the building, a tradition for all faculty and seniors. It was silly, perhaps, but Tyler appreciated the intention that simple action set for the entire day ahead.

He strolled into the school, the hallways abandoned, the

lights not even turned on yet. He passed the main office, seeing the lights in the back of the room turned on, likely Principal Ambrose enjoying his morning coffee while poring over the daily news sites. The faculty knew to leave Ambrose alone for this morning ritual, his desire to chat slowly ramping up with each sip of coffee he took.

Tyler continued forward, his classroom toward the end of the long hallway that connected the front lobby to the cafeteria on the opposite side of the building. He always had one final reminder of Amelia during his morning trip to class, passing the classroom that once belonged to Mrs. Floyd, Tyler's teacher who had been slain before the morning bell, her body drained of blood that spread across the room, only to be first discovered by Tyler.

He shook his head as he passed, refusing to make eye contact with the door. "Not today," he muttered, zipping by and entering his classroom. He somehow tiptoed through the minefield of memories without having a mental breakdown, now ready for the day ahead.

2

The ground shifted and heaved, then exploded outward, dirt flying in every direction. A frigid blast of air came with it, and Amelia Doss found her incorporeal body shot into the air above her own grave. Confusion set in. She did not know how long she'd been asleep, but when she pulled her arms in front of her, nothing was there. Her physical body had long since succumbed to decomposition. Nothing remained in the grave below except bones. She closed her nonexistent eyes, willing herself to float to the ground, her body coming together into something more solid. This time when she held up her hands in front of her face, she saw her pale fingers by the light of the moon.

It was a strange sensation, being a spirit. A wry smile slid over her lips as she let her hands fall to her sides and she looked around. She knew this was the family cemetery in the hills of Ridgeway, near the old mine. Her old house, long gone, was less than a quarter-mile down the hill. She'd gone to the new house once and killed the old woman there. Then it all came racing back to her. Her attempts at killing Tyler Reynolds, a descendant of Randall Nelson. *No,* she corrected herself. *He* was *Randall Nelson*. She looked at her hands again. They were nearly solid now. She felt the breeze on her face and in her hair, though she couldn't tell if it was cold or warm. She could feel the forest floor beneath her feet, but the sensation was different.

That's when she sensed him. The Reynolds boy. He was close. She had no way of knowing how long they had confined her to the grave, or what had released her. One thing was certain — she'd failed in getting her revenge. Her eyes narrowed. *Danny Espinoza*.

Danny had a natural gift for necromancy, one he kept using to toy with her. Well, she'd get him. Perhaps. In the distance, she heard the mine beckoning her. It was time for her to figure out what had gone on while she was asleep and to summon the shadows. She knew one thing for certain: this time she needed to finish the job. No messing around.

The short trek up the mountain to the mine seemed shorter than she remembered, though now being able to shed her physical body made traveling much easier. Faster, even. She could move through the air with greater efficiency and grace, not even having to go around objects since she could slide right through them. This gave her an advantage, and now she knew how the shadows could make quick work of most things, and even turn solid when they so chose. Amelia and the shadows were kin now, with the same abilities and same appearance, unless she coalesced into physical form. She reached the mine and willed herself solid again. The entrance was still sealed from the first time she'd returned from the grave. Did she pry it open with supernatural strength? Or did she shift right through the solid wood?

There was a crack behind her as a stick broke under the weight of something heavy. "Amelia," a voice whispered.

She turned toward the voice, only to find a large shadow standing there, its red eyes shining in the darkness. This shadow was new and bigger than most of the others. Amelia didn't know it yet, but she was always up to making new acquaintances. "Well, hello," she said, her voice echoing, carried by the wind. "I've never seen you among my shadows before. You're new."

The shadow drifted toward her. "I am Azazoth."

"How do you know me?" She tipped her head to examine him better, noticing the obvious wings and tail of his form.

"We share some friends," he said, his voice so sweet that it gave her pause. But only for a second.

"Then we shall be friends, too," Amelia told it with a bright smile. The shadows had never had names before, and she liked it. It made it easier to address a specific shadow, though she had many shadow friends and the thought of trying to remember all their names sent her head spinning.

Azazoth smiled, too, a thick, clear plasma dripping from his gleaming white fangs.

Her tone turned serious then. "We must summon the others. There is much to be done."

The shadow that looked like chaos itself merely nodded, that Cheshire cat grin still plain on his smoky face.

Amelia turned back to the entrance of the mine, still debating whether to rip the plywood from the framing of the entrance.

"Summon them first," Azazoth hissed behind her.

She whirled around to find the creature hovering over her shoulder. "Very well." Turning toward the forest, she lifted her now semi-opaque arms and called to them. "Come to me, my friends. Come." Her voice, carried on by the wind, reached out into the night, calling all manner of shadowed creatures to her. They came by the multitude. These creatures had become plentiful in a world of chaos, rage, and pain. So many came to her call, in fact, that they formed a solid wall of darkness around her and Azazoth. They whispered among themselves, their voices like a thousand snakes hissing.

"Silence!" Azazoth commanded.

The din died down and Amelia now held their full attention. "We have much to do. Tyler Reynolds is still alive, and they imprisoned me in my grave thanks to the witch, Danny Espinoza."

The shadows reacted exactly as she expected them to. They were appalled at such an affront to their mistress. For the first time since rising again, she felt warmth. It was Azazoth's hot, sulfuric breath in her ear. "What are we going to do about it?"

Amelia let out a maniacal giggle. "We're going to kill Tyler, of course."

"But how? The witch is too strong," one of the nameless shadows protested.

"Never mind Danny, for the moment. This time I won't spend as much time saving those around him from life. Though a girl and her shadows still must eat," she said.

Cackles of laughter coursed through the solid wall of writhing shadows.

"However, there are things we must do first to gain our bearings."

"Such as?" Azazoth asked.

"First, we must make a home of the mine. This is a place of power for me." She paused to make sure they were all still paying attention. "Second, we must discover how long I've been asleep. It will help me regain my footing. Third, I require something warm to sup on. Finally, we find Tyler so I can finish the job. I will not rest until he is dead and in the ground, deep beneath my bones."

A chorus of agreement ran through those assembled. There was a sickening snap behind her and she turned in time to see Azazoth remove the plywood from the mine's entrance as easily as one might snap a twig. *Azazoth is going to be extremely helpful,* she thought with pleasure. Sure, most of the shadows were adept at completing their tasks, but Azazoth, more than any of the others, had initiative. She knew they would become remarkably close friends.

With the mine now open, Amelia stepped into the cool darkness, breathing in, or rather experiencing the remembrance of breathing in, the earthy smells of the mine. She withdrew deeper into the tunnel, beyond the point where light from the outside could reach, and for the first time since her last resurrection, she felt at home. The shadows entered behind her, like guests seeing one's lodgings for the first time. By the sound of it, she gathered they were content with their new headquarters.

"What are your plans after we slay Tyler?" Azazoth asked.

"True rest and slumber. Never to be woken again," she whispered. The idea of eternal slumber was so close she could touch it. That's all Amelia wanted. Revenge and peace.

"Indeed," Azazoth said. His speech even had a different cadence than the other shadows. It was more refined. More intelligent.

Pleased with the fact that the mine was once again hers, Amelia found herself growing tired. She needed food, needed sustenance. Ridgeway, in its own way, provided that. They still spoke her name here, and she had a place in the Ridgeway Museum. It wasn't enough, though. She would have no choice but to kill a few others, not just Tyler, if only for the belief in her it would spark. She needed to feed on that belief to make her strong enough. But she also craved the blood. The metallic warm taste of it. The raw flesh of animals. Her favorite, of course, being human.

"Two birds, one stone," Azazoth said. Like the other shadows, she was mind-linked to him. But strangely, while he could sense her thoughts, she couldn't read his.

"Yes," she agreed. She narrowed her eyes again and peered at Azazoth, her head cocked to the side. "Why is it that, now that I'm a shadow, I don't have all of your abilities?"

"Such as?" he asked for the second time that night.

"You can read my thoughts, but I can't read yours."

The shadow laughed, its lopsided grin exposing that mouthful of razor-sharp teeth. "It will come."

Amelia clapped her hands together with delight. "Excellent. Now, I must eat."

She slipped around Azazoth and through the throng of shadows filling the cave until she found herself back outside, under the cool night sky. The stars were dimmer, it seemed. When she'd been alive, the night sky sparkled with stars so bright that one could see by them. Now, the light pollution of the cities blocked out their light, dimming the vast heavens above. She let out a wistful sigh and looked around her forest. The trees had all changed. Old growth had died back, and trees had fallen, only to be replaced by Nature herself with fresh growth and new plants. One thing in a century or more hadn't changed though – that Randall and his cronies put her to death in the most horrific of ways. Sure, she'd saved a few souls and rid the world of unsavory people before she went, but it had all been for the better good. It was her duty to do so. The shadows, often just their voices, had told her to do it. That a *just* deity would reward her hard work and diligence. But then came along Randall Nelson and his band of thugs who couldn't see the righteous work Amelia did.

Her hatred for Tyler surged. From the corner of her eye, she caught a movement in some underbrush a few yards away. She crouched down, easing toward the creature in silence until she was right on top of it. The rabbit never knew what hit it. Amelia snatched it up by the ears and brought it to her mouth, willed her teeth solid and ripping out the creature's neck in a single bite. The pathetic beast kicked as she gnawed at it, finally dying once it had lost enough blood.

She spit out the fur and chewed on the flesh, supping on the warm blood as it oozed from the wounds her teeth had inflicted. Even the mere act of life slipping away from such a small animal gave her some strength.

"It's a combination. Darkness must feed, and there is more than one way to feed," Azazoth said from behind her.

Amelia stopped eating and turned to him. Azazoth could prove quite useful, yes. He appeared to know a great deal about Amelia's current state, and how to gain strength. She wondered then what else he knew. Undoubtedly, there was much to be gained with Azazoth around. She smiled at her new friend. "What else should I know about my current state of existence?"

"In time," Azazoth said. The shadow put his arm around her like an old bosom buddy. "There is so much I have to teach you."

Smiling, Amelia offered the rabbit up to Azazoth. The shadow joined her in her meal.

Little did she know that while Azazoth planned to do as she asked and teach her what he knew, he also had plans of his own.

3

"Amelia Doss!" a voice shouted from the museum's entryway. Three boys, aged ten to fourteen, raced across the room in a stampede of footfalls toward the Amelia Doss display.

A startled Danny Espinoza was seized with fear and jumped, startled by the cry, then let out a sigh of relief when he realized the newcomers were just a few kids. He glanced over at Maryanne, who stood behind the register near the entryway collecting money from visitors. With a long look at the old scythe in his hand, he finished dusting it with a dry microfiber cloth and placed it back in the display case.

The boys' caretaker, presumably their mother, ambled over to the kids, who were busy pointing at the informational plaques. If they only knew how terrifying Amelia had really been. Danny sometimes wondered if having the exhibit was tempting fate.

He put on a wide smile and strode over to the rowdy bunch. "Do you have any questions?"

The mother smiled. "They're at that age where they love

horror films," she said. "When I told them that Ridgeway had their very own murderer, they insisted I bring them down here."

Danny nodded. Working at the Ridgeway Museum was only a part-time volunteer gig. He made his living writing novels now, and two of his most recent books were on the *New York Times'* bestseller list. "Indeed." He looked at the boys. "I happen to be an expert in the history of Amelia Doss, if you boys have any questions."

"Ooh, ooh!" The youngest raised his hand and jumped up and down.

He couldn't help but chuckle. There was probably a time in his pre-adolescence where blood and gore excited him, too, though he couldn't rightly remember. "Yes?"

"Did she kill people in their sleep?" the boy asked.

The oldest boy scoffed. "Probably."

"Amelia Doss got away with a lot of murders before they caught her. She's one of the first recorded serial killers in Colorado," Danny told them.

"Girls can't be serial killers," the older boy said, matter-of-fact.

Danny laughed. "While it's rarer for women to be serial killers than it is for men, even women can be psychopathic. But back then we didn't have psychological profiles. Thanks to sexism, our forefathers didn't realize a woman could be violent, let alone kill people twice her size."

The boys went silent. "She killed guys, too?" the oldest boy asked, his voice subdued and eyes wide with horror.

He nodded. "She killed older women, her own parents, her husband, her two children, and a few other people. Finally, a man named Randall Nelson and his friends, who'd later be deputized by the sheriff, were able to catch her. They hung her from a tree, underneath which she's now buried."

"Is she still there?" the youngest boy asked.

A cold chill ran up Danny's spine. He nodded with certainty. "She's still there. Buried near the family plot, but separate. She wasn't buried on hallowed ground." The children went silent and in that second, Danny could have literally heard a pin drop. He continued. "Back in those days, it was a common practice to bury the murderers and bad guys in graves separate from regular people."

The mother shuddered and folded her arms over her chest. "Well, that's creepy."

Danny couldn't disagree with her, so instead, he used their attention as a teaching moment, telling them all about how Ridgeway had been an old mining town, and how the world was a crueler place back then. "Amelia Doss may have just been a victim of her environment. Women didn't have the power and respect men had back then. They were frequently abused. In Amelia's case, it probably drove her to kill. It's also likely she had a psychological disorder of some sort, and since psychology was still in its infancy back then, she went undiagnosed," he finished.

The older boy nodded. "I bet Freddy, Jason, and Michael were also crazy."

His brow furrowed with momentary confusion.

"Freddy Krueger, Jason Voorhees, and Michael Myers," the boy impatiently explained.

Danny chuckled again when he realized the boy was talking about cinema's famous serial killers from the eighties. "Probably," he agreed.

Once the questions died down and Danny showed the boys a few artifacts from Ridgeways' mining days, the family left, leaving Danny and Maryanne alone in the museum once more.

"Lively bunch," Maryanne said, dusting off her counter. There was certainly no shortage of dust in the museum, and it seemed to Danny that three-quarters of the time he was at the museum, he spent it straightening, dusting, sweeping, and mopping. But he didn't mind. It got him away from the computer. Now that his books had become bestsellers, there was the constant pressure to make each new book as good as, or better than, the last. The Ridgeway Museum was where he came to relax and decompress when he wasn't on the road for a tour.

"Yeah, well, hopefully I taught them something," he said, a hint of hope in his voice.

Maryanne, who was in her late fifties, smiled at him. "You have a way of moving customers from our local legends to the real history, that's for sure." She looked at the back wall housing the Amelia Doss exhibit. "I hate that exhibit. I really wish they'd take it out of here."

"Well, it *is* part of the town's history, whether we like it or not. I imagine people in Lake City, home of the Alferd Packer museum, probably feel the same way," he said.

"We're not nearly *that* big of a tourist spot," she said with a shrug. "I've always looked at this place as a beacon of mountain mining history, marred by *that*." She motioned to the Amelia Doss exhibit.

Danny nodded. There was no point arguing with her. Maryanne, who'd been volunteering at the museum for as long as Danny could remember, had her opinions that would never change. Despite everything he and his best friend, Tyler Reynolds, had been through, he didn't mind the exhibit, even though there was a time in his life he probably felt the same way as Maryanne. When Amelia resurrected, the museum merely fueled people's fear and belief in the legend to give Amelia power. But it had been fifteen years since they put Amelia back in her grave for good, and all had been silent since.

"So, what are your plans for the night?" Maryanne asked. He knew she hated silence, so she resorted to small talk. It was the same conversation they always had near closing time.

"Same old thing. I'll probably grab a bite to eat at the diner, then head home to write a chapter." His eyes searched the large one-room museum for something to keep him occupied. More dusting, perhaps. "What about you?"

"Well, my daughter is bringing the grandkids over tonight to stay with me for a few hours so she and Larry can have a date night." Maryanne moved over to the longest wall, checking the straightness of the hanging artifacts.

"That sounds nice," he said. "By the way, is it true we're getting an old mining cart?"

That perked Maryanne right up. "Yes, though I honestly have no idea where we're going to put it." Her eyes went back to the Amelia Doss display. "Perhaps we should decrease the Doss display by half and put the mining cart right here in the corner. With a rope around it. We don't want the kids crawling on it."

"Good idea. You should definitely run it by the curator," Danny suggested.

She nodded.

Danny watched her go from display to display, checking to make sure everything was in its rightful place. Maryanne had been in Ridgeway when the murders started all over again. But like so many people, she thought the rash of murders was coincidental and that the rumors of Amelia Doss' return were inspired by the local legend. She never brought it up, and neither did he. "You realize there is literally nothing for us to do today. Perhaps we should start closing up." He glanced at his watch. It was almost five. "You can head out and I'll do it," he told her.

Maryanne let out a heavy sigh. "I suppose you're right. Let me just close out the register." She let no one close out the register during her shifts.

"Okay." Danny grabbed the big dust mop and went over the floors. By the time he finished, Maryanne had closed out, and they both left the museum, locking the door behind them. Danny didn't bother taking his car. He walked across the street and down two blocks to the local diner.

Elkhorn Diner was a dive, but Danny enjoyed the ambiance of the place. It was good for people-watching, something he enjoyed immensely. He sat in his usual corner booth so he could look out over the sea of people. He'd met a lot of interesting folks here. Even though Ridgeway was growing, with new developments springing up on the edge of town, it was still a smallish town. Not so much that everyone knew who everyone was, but small enough that if you sat in the diner for an hour or more, someone you knew would walk in. Tonight was no different. He'd just finished his eggs and hash browns when an old high school classmate walked in. The guy recognized him right away.

"Danny Espinoza!" the man greeted. He was in his thirties and thin, with a receding hairline.

"Hey bud. I'm sorry—remind me of your name," Danny said, putting out his hand.

The man grasped it and shook. "Josh Parker."

"Right. Football team?"

"Yeah, was a friend of Bryson Day's."

Danny nodded, the memory of having seen Bryson with Josh flooding back to him. Back then, Josh had considerably more hair. And muscles. "Ah, I remember."

"So I hear you're some big-time writer now. What do you write?" Josh sat down uninvited.

He dreaded that question, but only because he heard it so often that he could parrot the answer in his sleep. "I write horror novels."

"Like scary stuff?" Josh nodded, not waiting for an answer. "I suppose you would, after all that shit you and Tyler went through in high school. Heard you had a hell of a time at Denver State, too."

"Roughest years of my life. But I don't write about what happened," he lied. He had several files on his computer with his writing about what had happened to them. Writing was therapeutic, but so far none of it had been turned into something publishable. His old screenplays from college went nowhere. He'd been told by agents that the screenplay was trite. A "rehash of every eighties horror film ever made". After several rejections like that, he'd shelved it. Nowadays, he worried that if he published he and Tyler's story, it would somehow resurrect *her* again. Besides, Tyler had suffered enough. Now, his best friend had a wife, kids, a stable job, and most importantly, he was happy. There was no reason to dredge up the past.

"Right. So, horror, huh?"

"My most popular series is about an FBI agent who gets wrapped up in terrifying paranormal cases."

"Nice." Josh nodded, seemingly at a loss for words.

"What have you been up to?" Danny gave him a wide smile in hopes they could get the subject off of him and onto other topics.

"Working at the brewery. It's a good job."

"Married?"

"Divorced," he said. "You?"

Danny shook his head. "Not yet, no. Kids?"

"A daughter. Twelve." Josh certainly wasn't much of a conversationalist. "I take it you have no kids?"

"No," Danny said. Well, that was it. They had nothing else even remotely in common.

Josh finally got up. "It was good talking to you, Danny. I should probably get back to my friends over there." He nodded toward a table of middle-aged guys. "Good seeing you!"

"Yeah, you, too." Danny breathed a sigh of relief. At least Josh hadn't wanted to talk at great length about Bryson's death or Amelia Doss. Let alone he and Tyler's narrow escapes from a crazed killer. He was used to it, though. As long as he lived in Ridgeway, people were going to ask questions.

4

Tyler had prepared for another day of class, growing frustrated as the students moved deeper into the semester. Only a handful of the teens held any semblance of interest in his lectures. He understood that history, as a subject, was perhaps the most difficult to make engaging, but he felt extra energized to deliver today's content. His books and notes lay scattered across his desk as the students filed in for the first class of the morning.

"Good morning, Mr. Reynolds," each student greeted as they made their way to their desks, unzipping their backpacks and opening notebooks and hefty textbooks.

Tyler grinned and nodded as the room filled. Once the class had completely settled in, he returned behind his desk and silently closed his notebooks and textbook, slamming the latter shut with authority, demanding the attention of everyone in the room.

"American history isn't all what you think," he said, staring down at his suddenly cleared desk. "Our lesson today is about the Sand Creek Massacre, a horrific event that happened here in our own state. Instead of going through the book, or summarizing the lesson, I thought we might just talk about it, and how stories like this seem to get brushed under the rug. Keep in mind who dictates how our curriculum is organized. This is a public school, and if you've been in public schools for all of your education, which I'd assume most of you have, then you have been subjected to learning about history the way our government wants you to."

Tyler paused and circled to the front of his desk, leaning back on it with his arms crossed as he gazed around the classroom, several students shifting in their seats as they sensed a potentially uncomfortable discussion.

"From the day you were born, you've probably been told this is the greatest country in the world. And I agree with that statement—don't think I'm here to sway you from that belief. But the fact is, we have a dark, depressing history that is rarely spoken of. They don't want you to know the murder and bloodshed that got this country where it is today. You might see the news today and hear about systemic racism, and think this is a new thing. The very foundation of America is ingrained with treating other human beings like roadkill. And it's usually validated because of money.

"Now, we've talked about the Gold Rush of 1849, but the hunt for gold never stopped. Ten years later, gold was discovered in the Rocky Mountains and sparked another rush of settlers from the east coast. As was the case everywhere, Native Americans lived on the land surrounding the area. Several treaties had already been agreed upon and signed, but the discovery of gold led to a desire by the United States government to renegotiate these terms, and essentially find a legal way to kick the Indigenous peoples off their land.

"After a lot of back and forth, a group of soldiers attacked a village of Native Americans while the men were away hunting. The official death toll of Native people is said to be between seventy and five hundred, but keep in mind, over four hundred soldiers arrived for this slaughter. I highly doubt they would bring that many people to kill seventy others. This utter disregard for human life is the greatest tragedy that has ever happened in the state of Colorado, and I'll bet you've never even heard of it until today."

Tyler stopped and took a sip from his water bottle on the desk. All eyes in the class focused on him, no one daring to look away. "Well, has anyone heard of this event?"

Head shakes moved around the room, no one speaking up —not even his top students.

"I'm not trying to kill your pride for this country. All I'm asking is that you take a deeper look into its history. Find something named after someone, look them up. The governor who instigated this slaughter was John Evans. He has a mountain named after him today. The president who approved the governor's request? You may have heard of Abraham Lincoln. I'll bet you didn't expect that.

"The worst part of all this is that there are hundreds, if not thousands, of stories similar to this. And you'll never hear about them unless you actively seek them out. History is rich and never-ending. Challenge yourself to learn something about the past daily. Start here in the state, even here in Ridgeway. Every town has its own history, and you're only stunting your understanding of the world by not learning about it."

Tyler's stomach sunk as these last words left his mouth, worried he might have opened a door he knew his students were longing for. Three hands shot up immediately, and he already knew where this was going. They had tried in the past to get him to talk, but he had now backed himself into a corner after challenging his students.

"Yes, Ms. Carson?" Tyler called on Emily Carson, one of his top students who rarely let her grades fall below an 'A' average.

"Mr. Reynolds, I don't mean to change the subject. We all know about the legend of Amelia Doss here in Ridgeway. Would you be able to give us any insight into that story?"

"Yeah," said Samuel Murphy, another student with his hand in the air. "Did she really come back to life and try to kill you?"

The tension in the classroom grew thick, everyone giving their undivided attention for perhaps the first time this semester.

You're in this too deep now, Tyler thought, flailing for any way to back out of this conversation, but running into brick walls every way he turned.

"Okay, class, I will discuss what I know about Amelia Doss, but let's try to keep this focused on the actual history, about which I know almost everything there is."

"You and your friend, right?" Samuel asked. "Danny Espinoza? The horror writer. He went to school here too."

"Well, you all seem to have a lot of the story already. Why don't you just tell me what you want to know?"

"We just want to know if it's true," Samuel continued, pressing the matter.

"Of course the story of Amelia Doss is true. She really slaughtered people around town for a brief span of time that sent Ridgeway into a tailspin. Several murders went unsolved until they were eventually tied back to Amelia, some that didn't even have proof, but it was convenient to pin it on her. Keep in mind the science back in the 1920s was nowhere near where we have it today. No DNA tests, minimal forensics. Police and detective work solved most murders, and many assumptions had to be made. Some of the murders tied to Amelia were done so simply because they fell within the time of her rampage. She used a pattern of murder that the others didn't show, but they still were attributed to her."

"How many is she *actually* responsible for?" Emily asked.

"An official count is believed to be eighteen murders, though you'll see her credited with anywhere between twenty and forty, depending on the source. But I've done plenty of digging into her past, and am confident with the number eighteen. There may be more that we've never heard of, but we'll never know."

"So if you've done so much research, then she really must have come back to life to kill you," Samuel prodded.

The heads in the classroom swiveled back and forth like they were watching a ping pong match, anxiously awaiting each question and answer.

Tyler attempted a response. "There are similarities between the attacks in Ridgeway that happened when I was in high school and the ones from the 1920s, but do you really believe she rose from the grave and came back to slaughter the town? Think about what you're saying. I may not be a science teacher, but I still understand facts and reality. The rumors that have been going around town are completely baseless. What we have is a copycat trying to live in the shadow of Amelia Doss."

"Then what did you see that night?" Emily asked, refusing to let this topic go. "We've all read the stories from your encounter, and everything makes it sound like it was Amelia Doss. Her grave had been dug out, her corpse never found."

Tyler didn't recall that bit of information having ever been shared, knowing Abbott wanted to keep it under wraps. It was possible, even likely, that word had slipped from someone in the police department in the years that had passed since then. "I'm not sure what you're referencing. All I did was rescue my mom. There were a series of murders going around town, my mom was taken, and I went to save her. We don't know who was responsible to this day, as the person who had kidnapped my mom escaped after the police showed up."

"But it was a woman, right?" Samuel asked, he and Emily

now serving as mock attorneys on behalf of the classroom for this pressing round of questioning.

"It was, yes, but that doesn't mean it was a resurrected corpse. I'm telling you guys, it was a copycat. Think about it, why hasn't anything happened in Ridgeway since then?" Tyler didn't dare mention the Amelia/Ella drama that had unfolded at his college campus in Denver, and knew for a fact that none of that information had ever made it back to the Ridgeway newspaper. "We had a copycat that year, she was nearly caught, and she hasn't shown her face since then. Whoever it was probably moved as far away from here as possible."

"Mr. Reynolds, with all due respect, we *know* there's more to it," Emily said. "There has been so much news coverage and articles into those murders when you were still a student, and one thing that stood out is that all the murders seemed to have a connection back to you, even if a minor one. All the way to your mother being kidnapped before the killings stopped. Your friend, your teacher—who you discovered, by the way—the convenience store lady."

Tyler raised his hands in the air, completely on the defense now. "Look, I know there is a lot of information out there about these killings, but none of you were there. I was. There are coincidences, yes, but that doesn't explain anything. And it certainly doesn't conclude that Amelia Doss rose from the dead to come back and kill everyone. Now, if you don't mind, perhaps we should get back to our discussion about Sand Creek."

"Our discussion is about horrific events in Colorado's history," Emily said. "Why do you suppose Amelia's murder rampage is never mentioned?"

"It's old. There was a lot of inconclusive information, and it has morphed into a legend more than an actual historical event. Besides, it doesn't affect people the way a slaughtering of Native Americans does. Amelia is a small-town serial killer —no one outside of Amelia herself will justify what she did. But the Sand Creek Massacre, I'll guarantee you can still find people today—thousands of them—who would agree the American government did the right thing by taking innocent lives. And that's where the importance of history comes into play. You must understand where we've come from as a society if you want any chance of changing the future. We are still fighting this battle against oppression today—we are *not* fighting Amelia Doss in Ridgeway. That chapter has been closed. And that's the difference between meaningful history and stories from the past."

The bell rang to signify the end of class, startling Tyler as he jumped. Sweat had formed around his forehead, his emotions getting the best of him. He had lost control over his classroom and paid dearly. The students, Emily and Samuel included, all snapped their notebooks shut and disappeared into the bustling hallways as if nothing had just happened. For them, their day simply continued to the next class.

For Tyler, however, the discussion of Amelia had agitated his mind to the point of him wanting to cancel his next class to get his thoughts back in order. He felt deflated, drained of all desire to complete the day still ahead. He'd push through, just as he had always done, but this served as a reminder of the pull Amelia Doss had over his soul. The mere mention of her name had the potential to hijack his day.

Just let it go, he told himself. *She's gone and never coming back.*

5

Former Sheriff James Abbott sat in a corner booth at the Elkhorn Diner, his regular meeting spot with Tyler Reynolds. They enjoyed lunch together once a month, ever since Tyler had moved back to Ridgeway, catching up on life, and always whispering about Amelia Doss.

James had retired from the police force one year ago after serving in Ridgeway for over forty years. The town threw a big celebration to commemorate Sheriff Abbott and honor his decades of service and even re-named the police station after him. They had closed down Main Street and set up a carnival event, complete with rides, food stands, and a Pin the Badge on the Sheriff game with a life-sized doll of James a bit too realistic for his liking.

Regardless, he enjoyed himself at the event and caught up with familiar faces from around town he hadn't seen in years. He shook hands and hugged the residents he had dedicated his life to protecting, and as expected, soon had regrets about retiring thanks to the silence and boredom that plagued him after his daily morning round of golf.

The chime above the door rang out when Tyler entered the diner, promptly finding James in their usual booth and waving before starting his way over. James grinned as he stood up to shake Tyler's hand, noticing an extra couple of gray hairs popping out on the young teacher's head.

"Reynolds, how are you doing?" James asked as they both sat down, Tyler promptly flipping open the menu he didn't actually need to look at.

"Been better, Sheriff. The other day my class grilled me about Amelia. They backed me into a corner, and I really had no way out. I suppose it was bound to happen eventually, but it still caught me off guard and I've been off ever since. You ever get that eerie feeling when you hear her name? Like she's still out there and will finally come back."

"I don't hear much of anything these days, unless it's coming out of my mouth. And I definitely don't talk to myself about Amelia Doss."

"I'm sure that time period pops into your head now and then."

"Sure, but never to the point of consuming my thoughts. Sitting around all day, alone, your mind wanders with no real direction. Be glad you have a wife and kids to keep you company in life. That's my only regret today, but no one tells you about the silence when you're a young cop just starting out. So many new officers fall into the trap of marrying their job and never put aside time for a social life. It's hurting me now."

"You haven't met any ladies out on that golf course? I'm sure there are plenty of older single women in town. Hell, I work with a couple. I'm sure I can set up a date."

James chuckled and took a sip from his steaming mug of coffee. "Oh, Reynolds, you make that offer to me every month, and my answer is still no. Thank you for trying. I wouldn't know the first thing about dating a woman these days, so I'll just stick to new hobbies. I've been watching re-runs of Bob Ross. Remember that guy? I'm going to buy some paint and an easel and try to follow along."

"Painting, huh? My grandpa used to dabble with the paint-brushes. It's a very therapeutic hobby, should do you some good."

"I suppose it will. How is that friend of yours? Espinoza. I've been reading his books—he's got quite the talent for storytelling. Scary as shit, but I guess that only makes sense."

James paused and hoped Tyler didn't realize he had stopped because Amelia Doss popped into his mind. Of course Espinoza wrote horrifying stories. He had lived them.

"Danny's doing good. He's really revamped the museum since becoming the town historian. You should check it out sometime."

James shrugged. "Maybe I will."

He had no intention of stepping foot in the Ridgeway museum. A small exhibit had been created for him personally, outlining his career as the longest-serving sheriff in town history. Just seeing himself as a piece of history made him feel dizzy. And dead. Dead people had exhibits in museums, espe-cially in small towns. *Amelia Doss on one side of the building. Me on the other. I'll just visit when I'm a ghost.*

"How are the kids?" James asked.

"Doing good. Wyatt is rocking kindergarten, Charlotte is finally done with diapers and teething—that whole phase of hell. Me and Avery are actually getting some sleep again."

The diner's waitress, a middle-aged woman named Kimberly, approached the table. "My two favorite guys," she said, pulling out her notepad. "What can I get you both to eat?"

"I'll have my usual, darling," James said, sliding over his unopened menu.

"Breakfast burrito for me," Tyler said. "Extra bacon, please."

"You got it. Should be ten minutes."

Kimberly spun around and left them in silence as Tyler grabbed the coffeepot at the center of the table and poured himself a cup. James noticed a particular distant aura swimming beneath Tyler's surface.

"She's really stuck in your mind, isn't she?" James asked.

"For now. I go through this in waves sometimes. I guess I always will, since I never saw her dead body. It's a far leap for me to assume she is no longer walking this Earth. Will she really leave me alone? I doubt it. Maybe she's just waiting until I'm an old, defenseless man. One day I'll be sitting on my porch, yelling at the kids to get off my sidewalk. One day it will be her, and there will be nothing I can do to stop her."

James chuckled. "Quite the imagination you got there, son. You sure it's not you writing those scary books?"

"Yeah, that's exactly what I need—more dark thoughts in my head."

James shifted in his seat, bracing himself to deliver a bit of news that might make Tyler's head spin. "I gotta confess something, Reynolds. I go up to that old mine at least once a week. I have to. For an old cop like me, how things unfolded that night in Old Lady Myers' basement—it's not something I can just shake off. She doesn't haunt me, but that I couldn't capture her does. You know what I mean?"

Tyler nodded, his eyes narrow and focused on the sheriff. "Sure—the unsolved case. Every cop has one, right?"

James grunted. "Maybe in the movies, but I definitely do. Then you called me when you were at college, and I felt so helpless. You guys were in trouble, and the Day boy's grave was dug up. We never found that body. Part of me expects to see it one day up at that old mine. Where else would she put it?"

James caught himself speaking of Amelia as if he had proof she had done it all, despite zero evidence suggesting so.

"Have you ever found anything up there?" Tyler asked, leaning forward.

"Not yet. It's as abandoned as ever and still boarded up. No new skeletons, no dead animals. I even left a slab of meat up there once, just to see what would happen. Had it inside a baggie and put it right inside the mine where most animals refused to go. The next week I went back, it was still there, spoiled and covered in mold."

"Interesting," Tyler said, leaning back and stroking his chin. "That doesn't make sense, either. There are animals in the woods, always have been. You'd think a bear or wolf would have taken their chances with the meat. Even a mountain lion. When we were wandering around that area as kids, there were always dead animal carcasses near the mine, even on the Myers property. Looking back, I'm pretty sure that was what Amelia was feeding on. The meat going untouched makes me wonder if she is still in the area and has scared off the animals."

"That seems like a stretch. Maybe the animals don't go near the mine because there's nothing there for them. It's one of the furthest points from the river."

"Even still, not even a fox or squirrel has wandered in that direction? A scavenger? It doesn't add up."

Kimberly returned with two plates of food and placed them in front of the men. "Anything else I can get for you two?"

"I think we're good, dear, thank you," James said, promptly unraveling his napkin and silverware. Kimberly grinned and turned away. "I see it in your eyes, Reynolds. Don't overreact to this. You're thinking too much about the details."

"Well, someone needs to. You're not involved anymore."

James raised a steady, yet stern, hand. "And everything has been just fine. No murders, no dead animals."

"Then what are you expecting to find at that mine? If you truly believed everything was fine, why waste your time climbing through those woods? Especially at your age."

James pointed a stiff finger at Tyler. "This old man can still kick your ass, Reynolds, and don't you forget that. I don't know what I'm hoping to see. It's been so long—I guess I just want closure."

"But she will be back. Don't you understand that? An evil creature like that will always return home."

James shrugged. "Then I hope it's long after I'm gone. Godspeed to whoever has to deal with that." He shoved a fork full of steak into his mouth.

"Let me go with you next time," Tyler said. "When are you going next?"

James gulped down the meat. "I don't think that's a good idea. You clearly have some issues to sort through with Amelia Doss. The mine will only trigger all those old memories. You still haven't come full circle from that tragic night with your mother—and the mine isn't going to do you any favors. Besides, I go in the mornings during the week. You have young minds to mold. This seems like a silly reason to take a day off."

"Maybe it is. But I want to see for myself. Maybe I'll notice something you didn't. Don't forget how much I have studied Amelia."

James squirmed in his seat. Reynolds raised a good point, especially since James didn't have a real strategy once he wandered into the woods. He had ever only hoped to find something obvious, like a corpse, or blood. Even a weapon. He'd never notice a subtle clue, especially with his mind virtually turned off from the heavy detective work it had been used to. *Use it or lose it,* he thought, knowing his skills had started to diminish the day following his retirement.

"Tell you what. I'll call you the next time I go up there. What time is your lunch break?"

"11:30."

"Perfect. I'll plan my trip for that time. I'll try to call you while I'm up there, but the cell reception is hit or miss—think it depends on the clouds. If anything, I'll call you when I'm done."

"Let's try to video chat while you're there."

"Reynolds, you know I'm not going to dabble with that technology bullshit. Be happy I know how to send you a text message."

Tyler laughed at this, but James didn't mean it as a joke. The world and technology moved a bit too fast for this retired small-town sheriff. He saw how everyone walked around town with their phones held in front of them, as if the little devices were guiding them to their next destination. No one ever looked up anymore, it seemed, everyone content to remain in their personal bubble as they moved through life with even less human interaction.

"I'll call you on the phone like a normal human being," James said.

They finished their meal, drifting away from the topic of Amelia Doss as they caught up on the happenings in the wide world of sports and entertainment. He'd never admit it, but James thought Reynolds might be on to something with his theory of the absent animal life near the mine. He'd pay closer attention the next time he visited.

$$\text{❧} \quad 6 \quad \text{❧}$$

Tyler was close. Amelia could feel it. His presence nagged at her, drawing her closer toward him. He wasn't near the oldest part of Ridgeway. Instead, his energy pulled her through the growing town to the opposite side and new housing development, where every house looked like the one next to it. It was cold and barren in its lack of distinctive design and pale colors. After she'd feasted on raccoon and squirrel, she and the shadows moved out, flying through the night like wraiths, invisible to those who never looked too closely into the dim doorways and obscure walkways. They kept to the in-between places that most humans avoided out of fear. Human instinct was strong. All Amelia could think was that there was a reason so many people feared the darkness.

Finally, they approached a house where Tyler's energy was strong and oozed from the earth and air with a specific scent. Azazoth remained beside her, an ever-constant companion whispering in her ear. "He's here," Amelia said.

"Yes," Azazoth agreed. Being a shadow of chaos, the glint of evil in his eyes never diminished.

They circled the house, a mass of gloom pulsating with intent, peering in windows, and watching as Tyler and his wife unpacked some boxes, his children, a little boy and an even younger little girl, content in playing on the living room floor.

"It's time for dinner," the woman with the long, dark hair said. She was, presumably, Tyler's wife.

"Pretty little thing," Azazoth whispered, his red glowing eyes peering through the bottom pane of glass through the dining room window. The bushes they hid behind shifted from Amelia and Azazoth's movement.

But Amelia had no interest in the wife or children. Her eyes focused on Tyler and how secure he seemed in the safety of his new home. Amelia and the shadows watched and waited. The family ate dinner and Tyler and his wife cleared the table afterward. It all seemed to happen so quickly. For Amelia and the shadows, however, time was irrelevant. They could have sat there, entrenched in the darkness for hours, and it would have seemed like mere seconds.

"Should we go in?" Azazoth finally asked, a hint of impatience in his voice.

A sly grin slid over Amelia's nonexistent lips. "We can live in the walls and closets where it's dark," she said.

The shadows, including Azazoth, hissed in agreement, a resounding "Yessss" like a thousand rattlesnakes in a cavern.

The woman paused and looked toward the window. Amelia instinctively ducked down, momentarily forgetting that she had shed her mortal coil. No longer did she have to worry about having a body if she didn't want it. Of course, she could also materialize if she chose. "Did you hear something?" the woman asked.

Tyler returned to the dining room. "What?"

"Outside. I thought I heard something." The shadows went dead silent.

"Crickets, maybe?"

"No, it sounded more like a weird buzz. Almost like voices, but more like an insect." She furrowed her brow and came right up to the window and peered out, likely seeing nothing in the night.

"Do you still hear it?" Tyler joined her at the window. "You can't see outside with the light on." He went back to the light switch and flicked it off.

Azazoth looked up, his eyes blazing and jaws hanging open, gleaming white fangs bared.

The woman screamed before Tyler turned around. He flicked the light on. "What?!"

"There was something, I think. In the bushes." She backed away from the window.

"What did it look like?"

"It had big teeth and creepy eyes."

"Come over here and turn off the light. I'll look," he said with a chuckle. "Probably a skunk or a raccoon."

She did as he instructed, turning off the light while Tyler came to look. This time, Azazoth ducked down with Amelia and snickered.

"There's nothing out here. It's dark, though. We'll get more outdoor lighting. That should keep the critters away." He looked around one last time. The light switch flicked back on.

His wife breathed a sigh of relief. "I'm probably just tired."

"Maybe you should let me finish up down here and you can take the kids up to bed. We'll call it an early night," he suggested.

She nodded. "Okay. Sounds good."

They kissed and embraced, then the woman went into the living room and ushered the two children upstairs. Tyler went back into the kitchen, turning off the dining room light behind him.

Amelia turned to Azazoth. "How shall we get in? Have the shadows slip in and unlock the door?"

"You forget yourself, Amelia. You are thinking like a flesh-and-blood creature again," Azazoth cooed. "We can slip in under the door, or through a vent."

A wave of excitement washed over her. She'd never been able to do that before, so this was a treat. She could go wherever she wanted, including into the walls where she could watch and listen. It would give her time to think about when and how to kill Tyler Reynolds. She slid around the side of the house, to the front door. But there was no space beneath it.

"Follow me," Azazoth said. He rose from the ground in a thin line of ethereal black smoke that wisped around the house until he found a vent leading into the attic. Amelia followed, dream-like in the sensation of floating. Together, they slipped in through the vent, their energy coalescing into more solid forms once they were inside. Below them, in the bedrooms, they could hear the mother reading to her children.

Amelia lowered herself to the beams and listened.

"Good night, moon," the woman said.

The children giggled. "Good night, moon," the little girl called out.

"I can't see the moon," the boy said.

"Well, it's there. Just invisible right now. Probably hiding behind some clouds," his mother told him. She let out a heavy sigh. "Okay, you two. Mommy is so tired. Let's just go to bed now, okay?"

"Can Wyatt sleep in here tonight?" the little girl asked.

"Why? You both have your own rooms now."

"I want to have a sleepover," the child said, hopefully.

"She's scared by herself sometimes," the little boy said. "Don't worry, Mom. I don't mind."

"Oh, alright. Then get into bed." There was a rustle of blankets. "But tomorrow night, Wyatt gets to sleep in his own room. Okay?"

"Okay," the little girl agreed. Then she said, "I'm not tired."

"I know you're not, but we all need our sleep. Otherwise, how will we get up in the morning for pancakes?" An edge of exasperation came through the woman's tone.

"Okay," came the girl's voice, defeated.

"I love you." Pause. "I love you." Then a click as the light went out. Then the rooms below went silent.

Amelia smiled and slid into the walls like a rat. She emerged into a closet with only a few children's outfits hanging in it. The door stood ajar and an eerie glow from the light plugged into the wall socket filled the room. Poking her head out, she saw the two still figures of the children.

There was a small gasp and the little girl, likely only three, jolted upright in bed and looked straight at her.

The child could see her. How could that be? She looked around for Azazoth, but he was nowhere to be found, though she could sense he was close. Probably slinking through the walls, getting the layout of the house. Amelia slipped back into the darkness of the closet, feeling her ethereal body for solidity. There was none. That's when the knocking in the walls began, and Amelia tried not to laugh aloud. Good old Azazoth, checking out the walls.

She heard a whisper from inside the bedroom. "Wake up."

"What?" the little boy groggily asked his even littler sister.

"There's a lady in our closet. I'm scared."

Amelia pushed open the door a bit and stuck her head out again, looking at the children with what she deemed a pleasant smile.

"That's her!" The toddler pointed at her.

Her big brother sat straight up in bed and pulled his sister back and behind him. "Who are you?"

"My name is Alice," Amelia said with a giggle.

There was some more knocking in the walls near the bed's headboard. They both jumped.

"Don't worry, that's just my friend Azzie."

"Do you live in the closet?" the little girl asked.

Amelia shook her head. "No. Me and Azzie live in the walls." She giggled again. Then she saw Azazoth emerge from the solid wall right behind the children. "Look, there's Azzie now."

The children whirled around on the bed. Azazoth smiled, his white fangs gleaming and his red eyes with the horizontal pupils wide. Both children let loose bloodcurdling screams that filled Amelia with delight. The door flung open, and a panicked Tyler and wife rushed into the room, flicking the lights on, only to find their children clutching each other tight, eyes squeezed shut.

"What happened?"

"There's a monster in Charlotte's room!" the boy shouted.

All the while, Amelia hadn't moved from her spot in the closet.

"There's a lady too," the girl said, pointing to the closet.

"Yeah," her brother agreed. "They live in the walls."

Tyler furrowed his brow with a flash of concern in his eyes, and then he sat at the edge of the bed, both children practically throwing themselves onto his lap. "I don't see any monsters."

"They're gone now," the boy said. "Can we sleep with you guys? Alice and Azzie are scary."

"Wait, the monsters have names?" Tyler seemed to be amused by his children's fear.

Amelia frowned.

His daughter nodded most emphatically. "The lady in the closet is Alice and her friend, the monster, is Azzie."

"And they live in the walls?" He glanced at his wife, who stood in the doorway.

"Ty, maybe we should just let them sleep with us. But only for tonight. Tomorrow night we'll arm you each with special monster spray, but Wyatt still sleeps in his own room." She clapped her hands together.

Tyler gave her a funny look. "Okay. Mommy has spoken. Into our room, but only for tonight. Tomorrow we'll formulate special monster spray."

The children grabbed blankets and pillows and hurried off to their parents' room across the hall, leaving the couple alone in the room. Tyler looked around again. "I wonder what brought that on."

"New house. Overstimulated." She shook her head and gave him a smile. "I'll give them spray bottles filled with water tomorrow night. They'll be fine."

He nodded and went to the closet, opening it all the way and flicking on the light.

Amelia was standing right there, in the darkest corner, but Tyler didn't see her.

"What are you doing?" his wife asked.

"Checking the closet for monsters, of course."

She laughed. So did he. They turned off the light and went to join their children in the master bedroom, leaving Amelia and Azazoth alone in Charlotte's room.

Azazoth began carefully stacking the plastic totes filled with toys in the middle of the room until they reached the ceiling. Then he moved two child-sized chairs from where they sat next to the wall, to the middle of the room.

"What are you doing?" Amelia asked the elder shadow.

"Let's go downstairs and do the same thing." Azazoth cackled with delight.

"For what purpose?"

"To scare them. Fear is good food," he said.

That made perfect sense to Amelia, so she followed him through the second floor, down to the first. They pulled all the dining room chairs out from the table, and they moved a chair in the living room from one side of the room to the other. When they'd finished, they slipped back up to the attic, laying down between the beams, whispering and laughing about how surprised and afraid the Reynolds family would be by morning.

Little did they know that while only the children could see them clearly, and Tyler's wife had caught a glimpse of Azazoth crouching in the flower bed, Tyler could hear their whispers through the ceiling. He lay below them staring at the ceiling, cocking his head from side to side trying to make out the words.

Amelia and Azazoth went quiet when they heard a noise below them.

"Tyler, did you hear that?" his wife asked.

"Yeah."

"It sounds like whispering."

"We could have mice," he said. "Don't worry. My mom is bringing the dog home tomorrow. If there are creatures living in the house, he'll find them and chase them off." Tyler sounded quite sure of himself.

Amelia and Azazoth began laughing, but Amelia stopped abruptly. "I don't like dogs."

"Neither do I." Azazoth grinned.

$\mathscr{H}$ 7 $\mathscr{H}$

The next morning, Tyler woke an hour before his alarm. He expected as much, the two kids taking all the space, their little bodies somehow pushing him and his wife to the edges of their king-sized bed. Aside from sleeping on the edge, he occasionally caught a foot or arm across the face. By 3 A.M. he debated sleeping in Wyatt's room to have any chance of uninterrupted sleep.

He never left, instead turning on his side and getting just comfortable enough to absorb the random kicks in his back instead of his face. It had another hour to fall back asleep. There were definitely sounds coming from the attic above, and while they sounded like whispers, he knew they were most likely the gentle gliding of rodent feet pattering around. As much as he hoped the dog might help scare away any critters, the attic was a different story. They'd need an exterminator to decide what options would be best to prevent the mice from returning. They'd need to address it today, before the mice built a nest and added to their population in the Reynolds household.

Saturday mornings typically consisted of cartoons for the

kids, while Tyler and Avery cooked a full breakfast. Thanks to their lack of quality sleep, everyone would enjoy a premium meal of Cinnamon Toast Crunch. With Tyler being the first up, he lay on the couch in the silent living room, unable to complete his journey to the kitchen, as his head grew heavier with each step. They had plans of painting their main-level bathroom to kickstart a remodeling project, but that likely wouldn't happen either. Sometimes, with kids, you had to take the loss and try again the next day.

He hadn't been on the couch for two minutes when the thud of feet hitting the floor upstairs startled him, the pitter-patter of little soles running down the hallway toward the stairs. Tyler felt all hope for a quick nap fade, and he shook his head as tears welled in his eyes. He couldn't recall the last time he had been this tired, but his brain itched with fatigue, his eyes heavy as boulders and surely bloodshot.

The kids rumbled down the steps, squealing as they bolted into the living room and jumped onto Tyler like starving puppies.

"Daddy!" Wyatt cried. "Mommy said you would make us breakfast. We want pancakes!"

"Pancakes, Daddy!" little Charlotte repeated, pulling herself onto the couch since she couldn't quite match the athletic leaps of her older brother.

"Sorry, guys, it's gonna be a cereal day. Maybe pancakes tomorrow."

"Awwww, but Daddy—" Wyatt began.

"Nope," Tyler interjected. "No begging—we're not dogs. Daddy's very tired, guys. Somebody was kicking me in the face all night."

Charlotte giggled.

"I promise, if I don't get kicked again tonight, I'll make pancakes tomorrow morning."

"*Magic School Bus!*" Wyatt shouted, completely losing interest in the breakfast topic.

"Ms. Frizzle!" Charlotte cried, hopping off the couch and sitting on the floor in front of the TV.

Tyler couldn't help but crack a grin. As crazy and exhausted the kids made him at times, it was always their simplest of actions that filled his heart to the brim. Seeing Charlotte sitting at complete attention facing the blank screen, her hair a frazzled mess, Tyler thought of his childhood doing the same thing, eager to watch the newest episodes of *Arthur* every Saturday morning.

Wyatt was equally excited, but clung to Tyler as he spun to reposition his body to face the TV.

"Before we turn on the TV," Tyler said. "Why don't you two tell me what happened last night. What scared you so badly? You think you saw a monster in the closet?"

"Not a monster, Daddy," Charlotte said, spinning around to face Tyler. "A lady."

Tyler's mind had been so consumed with Amelia over the past week, that she naturally jumped to the front of his thoughts. They were surely beyond the point of her toying with Tyler. If she was indeed back in Ridgeway, her eyes would be set on finally killing him. No fluff. No distractions. That had burned her in the past, and he was grateful for it. He tried to shove her out of his thoughts, also acknowledging that children of this age could develop imaginary friends.

"What did she look like?" Tyler asked. "And you saw her, too, Wy?"

Wyatt nodded.

Kids don't see the same imaginary friend, Tyler thought. *Maybe it was just the shape of something in the closet.*

Tyler had mistaken objects in the dark plenty of times, his hyperactive mind trying to make them into something much darker than a broom handle or puffy coat.

"We didn't see her too good," Charlotte said.

"Yeah," Wyatt said. "It was dark. But she talked to us."

"Did she come out of the closet?" Tyler asked.

"She stayed inside," Charlotte said.

"Did she tell you her name?" Tyler asked, bracing himself for a potential answer that would cause him to put the house up for sale today and move the hell out of Ridgeway.

Wyatt and Charlotte looked at each other, trying to rack their young brains for the already distant memory.

"Alice!" Wyatt said, sticking his finger in the air proudly.

"Alice," Charlotte repeated.

Alice, Tyler thought. *Close, but not mistakable.*

"Are you sure?" he asked, desiring complete confidence in their answers. He debated asking them specifically if the girl in the closet might have called herself Amelia, but decided it was best to never speak that name aloud in front of the kids. At least until they were adults and could handle hearing the horrific events from his adolescence.

"Yes, Daddy," Wyatt said. "Her name was Alice, and her friend was Azzie."

"Friend? You didn't mention anything about that?"

"Azzie was scary," Charlotte said. "Azzie the shadow man."

"He lives inside the walls," Wyatt said nonchalantly.

Tyler didn't know what to think, but felt better hearing about a friend. Nothing he had ever read—or experienced— about Amelia suggested she had friends with her. The name Azzie didn't ring a bell, either.

"How did you see Azzie if he lives inside the walls?" Tyler asked, desperate to put his mind at ease.

"He came out of the walls when Alice asked him to," Wyatt said.

"Alice said he was nice," Charlotte added. "But he looked very spooky."

"So you saw him better than Alice?"

"He had red eyes and pointy teeth," Wyatt said. "Can we watch *The Magic School Bus* now?" He had grown bored with this conversation, Tyler more concerned than his son.

Avery heard sounds in the walls last night, as did Tyler, but mice were still the rational explanation, certainly not a shadowy figure who could walk through walls.

"Not yet, guys, sorry. I just need to know everything. Remember, me and Mommy have to check under your bed and in your closet for any monsters. We need to know what kind we should be looking for so we can pick them up and throw them outside."

Charlotte giggled at the visual. "Azzie was a monster. Alice was not. She was a nice girl."

"Well, I didn't think she seemed nice," Wyatt said, crossing his arms. "She scared me, too. I don't want to ever see her again."

"Me and your mom will check your rooms and make sure there are no more monsters, okay?" Tyler stood up and grabbed the remote to turn on the TV. "In fact, I'm gonna go check them right now, so we don't have to worry about it the rest of the day. Sound good?"

"Yes, Daddy," Charlotte said, hanging her head low. Tyler wondered if she was actually disappointed that Alice would not be returning and shook his head at the thought. Sometimes kids had the most off-the-wall logic and all you could do was shake your head.

"Okay, you two—watch your show, and I'll go check your rooms. Then I'll come back down to make breakfast."

"Yay!" Charlotte cried, her mood shifting instantly.

The kids had checked out from the conversation about Alice and Azzie, already lost in the world of *The Magic School Bus* as Tyler broke away and slipped up the stairs to Charlotte's bedroom.

He entered, and his heart skipped a beat. An icy chill ran

the length of his body. In the center of the room, Charlotte's toy chests had been piled high to the ceiling, something neither Charlotte nor Wyatt could have done. The toddler's desk chair and rocking chair had been put in the middle of the room, just like he'd found all the chairs downstairs that morning. He unstacked the totes and placed them against the wall again, and then moved the chairs back.

With a deep breath, he turned and looked at the room. Charlotte's bedsheets were twisted and thrown in every direction. The closet in question had the door ajar, so Tyler moved toward the bed to see the angle the kids had viewed when they had shouted last night. Through the crack in the doorway he only saw darkness, and supposed in the middle of the night, things might have appeared differently.

Tyler sat at the foot of Charlotte's bed directly across from the closet door. His mouth dried up as his eyes remained locked on the closet. The room was silent, no sounds coming from within the walls or ceiling.

A cool draft moved over him, sending gooseflesh up his back, each hair standing stiffly on his neck.

"Amelia?" Tyler called out, just above a whisper, half-expecting the resurrected serial killer to kick open the closet door and charge toward him.

No such thing happened, yet his heart beat faster, and sweat formed on his forehead and palms as he continued his stare down against the closet door.

Get a grip, he thought. *She hasn't been in Ridgeway, and certainly hasn't been in your house. If she was, you wouldn't be here.*

As much as this may have been true, Tyler couldn't accept the possibility that he was ever safe. Until he saw Amelia back in her grave with his own eyes, why should he? She had already proven to possess supernatural abilities. Was living in the walls too far out of reach for her, or was it a cakewalk?

A knock came from the bedroom door, startling Tyler as

he jumped off the bed and snapped back into reality. Avery stood in the doorway, wrapped in her robe as she studied her husband with a look of confusion.

"Is everything okay?" she asked, stepping inside the room.

"Yeah. The kids are watching their show downstairs. I told them I'd check their rooms for the monsters that scared them last night." He decided not to mention anything about the totes or chairs. There was no reason Avery or the children should feel unsafe.

Avery giggled, brushing her hair aside. "Any luck?"

"Not yet, no monsters are showing themselves to me."

"Well, you are such an intimidating man, I don't blame them."

Tyler had been bottling up his concerns and growing fear of Amelia Doss, but had yet to mention it to his wife. He didn't want to scare her, especially over something that had an incredibly high likelihood of not being relevant. Unfortunately, meeting with Sheriff Abbott once a month wasn't enough for Tyler to get what he needed off his chest. He had a family to consider and would have to go through his days as if everything was fine. He believed it possible the kids may have heard something in the closet, maybe they even saw a ghost. His dark past with Amelia allowed him to accept such a wild thought.

"I'm sure they just heard the wind or something," Tyler said. "Sometimes the shed door outside comes unhinged and bangs against the wall. I'll check it out today. Ready for breakfast?"

Tyler pushed by his wife to exit the bedroom as quickly as possible. He wanted to give the appearance of confidence in what she likely perceived as a typical childish reaction the kids might have had. He'd need to find time to slip away and dig into his old documents and research on Amelia and look for any connections to the names Alice or Azzie.

⚜ 8 ⚜

James Abbott popped a cigarette into his mouth as he sat behind the wheel of his Dodge pickup. He had given up the daily habit after he retired from the force. Smoking had helped curb the stress of the job, and now that the stress was absent, he grew fond of trying new teas, sodas, and an occasional cigar on the golf course as his main vices in life.

Whenever he ventured up to the mines, though, a cigarette was the only thing that could settle his nerves. As a former sheriff, James trusted the evidence that suggested Amelia had not been back to Ridgeway since she left fifteen years ago. But as a man, and child of the small mountain town where local legends ran rampant, he half-suspected Amelia watched him from the woods each time he visited the mines. And one day, she just might jump out and end his life, leaving him as dead as the squirrels she used to kill and eat.

It wasn't even death that terrified him the most—that he could handle and accept. What kept him up at night was thinking of a potential encounter with Amelia, locking eyes with her deadly gaze, and not being able to warn anyone that she was indeed back in town. It was a helplessness he couldn't grasp, a reality he prayed to never have to encounter.

James had parked on the property that once belonged to Old Lady Myers, the house still abandoned all these years later after the gruesome murder discovered in the basement by Tyler and Danny. The home had been listed for sale for the last twelve years, but the only people who stopped by were out-of-town visitors hoping to spot paranormal activity.

The locals reported never reported anything suspicious coming from the house, despite the legend that preceded it. James stepped out of his truck and crushed his cigarette butt under his boot, staring at the house he hadn't been inside of since that incident. The windows had become opaque with dust. Ivy climbed up the exterior and even appeared to break through the siding in certain spots. Weeds that grew up to James' knees had overthrown the small patch of grass and flower beds that Old Lady Myers used to care for. Chunks of the wooden siding had deteriorated, falling to the ground below. The house had maybe another decade before it would collapse into itself. A heavy snowstorm could be the final blow to break a hole through the roof and cause mayhem inside.

James blew out the final smoke he had held in his lungs before trudging through the weeds to the back of the house. The graves of the Doss family remained a couple hundred yards behind the house, and he always stopped by them first before beginning the hike to the mine.

He moved through the weeds and tall grass that decorated the back of the property, approaching the row of graves within three minutes. "Good morning, Doss family," he greeted the gravestones, Amelia's still peppered in graffiti. James crouched in front of hers and felt the ground, making sure nothing had been dug out. The dirt was hard and compact, not a sign of tampering to be seen, unless you counted the weird hole, about an inch in diameter, that was in the center of the plot. *Probably a mouse or snake,* he thought. Reaching down, he picked up a flat rock about three inches in diameter and placed it over the hole, as if that would stop anything from getting in or out.

He stood and brushed his hands free of the dirt, shaking his head. "You sure are causing a lot of headaches for some of us," he said, patting the ground with the sole of his boot to confirm the earth's firmness. "I don't know what to believe these days, but I'd much appreciate if you left us a sign that you will no longer haunt this town. We're all ready to move on, and hope you are, too."

James snorted, realizing he had never spoken to Amelia's gravestone before, feeling childish, and guilty, for doing so.

"Rot in hell," he muttered under his breath, as if fearful Amelia might overhear it and reach right out of the ground to squeeze the life out of his throat. James broke away from the graves and continued up the mountainside, the old mineshaft another five hundred yards away.

Retirement had led to him being in the best physical shape of his life. He had replaced daily coffee and baked goods with tea and golf. And now this occasional hike to check on the mine. Being an officer in a small town didn't require physical prowess. Only once in his career did he have to run someone down by foot. He'd exerted his strength multiple times when de-escalting a rowdy drunk at a bar, but the perpetrators were rarely bigger than James himself.

He wore his holster when venturing into the woods, and patted his pistol to make sure it was still there. James brought it in case he encountered any bears or mountain lions, but he knew deep down it was there for Amelia Doss. He'd never seen a bear in the woods, despite them venturing into town once a year and causing mayhem for the residents hiding in their homes. As for mountain lions, he supposed they lived further up the mountain, as he couldn't recall having ever seen one during his life in Ridgeway. For all he knew, they didn't even roam the area.

It's for you, Amelia, and I ain't afraid to use it.

James marched up the mountain, a tinge of fear creeping up his back as it always seemed to once he was out of sight from his truck. Alone in these woods, anything could happen to him and no one would ever know. There were even more legends that reached beyond Amelia Doss within these mountains. Once the mine was built, people rarely ventured beyond it, but history suggested more events had taken place further up the mountain.

Old Native American artifacts had been discovered in the area, along with a couple of skeletons. Shortly after the mine had opened, the trail that led from the mine toward the top of the mountain had become known as Suicide Row. The isolation provided plenty of privacy for people to come take their lives without distraction. There had been an influx of missing person reports during the Great Depression, and they discovered most of those bodies in this remote part of the woods.

The area had a wicked history, and James would take no chances when roaming the grounds. That Amelia had risen from the dead to haunt the town once more seemed an appropriate, if not destined, way to show what the cursed area was capable of.

The breeze ruffled the leaves high above, the echoes sounding like distant voices whispering, keeping the woods' darkest secrets. The way the sounds bounced around always made James stop in his tracks to make sure he wasn't being followed, and this time was no different. He came to a halt and leaned against the nearest tree, catching his breath and spitting on the ground.

Left my water bottle in the car, he thought, shaking his head and licking his lips. Thirst attacked much quicker thanks to the higher elevation, but he was fortunate the trip was a short one.

James continued, able to see the front entrance of the mine roughly fifty yards away, picking up the pace as he wanted to get this trip over with. The last leg of the climb was steepest, and by the time he reached his destination, he hunched over his knees and gasped for air.

"Fuck," he wheezed. "Getting too old for this shit." His calves and hamstrings burned, and the only thing keeping him from lying down for a two-hour nap was knowing it was all downhill when he finished.

After a minute of letting his heart and breathing rates settle to manageable levels, James stood up straight and gazed to the mine entrance, his jaw hanging open. "No fucking way."

They had boarded the entrance shut after the bodies were found fifteen years earlier, during Amelia's last rampage through town. The job wasn't completed to perfection, several slots remaining open, big enough to stick an arm through. But it still served its job to keep humans and creatures out of it. James had even stuck the bait he'd left in the past through the slots, but never so much as claw marks appeared on the wooden boards.

Today the boards had been cracked down the center, appearing as if they had been blasted by a bomb, or even a bulldozer, some even ripped away. Even in the warm daylight, chills and gooseflesh ran up James' back as he stood there, mouth agape. He knew what it meant, even as his mind raced to find any other reasonable explanation.

A quick phone call and request for a favor could deliver him information if the city had authorized any recent changes to the mine. But it didn't have the looks of an intentional destruction—someone had clearly broken their way through.

He took a step closer, craning his neck to see into the darkness of the mine, unable to make out anything, as the sun's angle wasn't quite where it needed to be. "Hello?" he called out in a shaky voice. "Anyone in there?"

His voice echoed, bouncing back to him like a boomerang. He gazed into the black hole, his hand sliding toward his pistol, waiting for Amelia Doss to emerge from the shadows.

He stood this way for an entire minute, his mouth growing dry with fear, sweat running down his face in silent streaks. Nothing came from the mine. Birds tweeted high in the trees above, mocking him with their cheerful, innocent tunes.

James took another step closer, now realizing the cross-roads right in front of him. He could either turn around, make some phone calls to report the damage at the mine, and never worry about it again. Or he could venture inside and look around, knowing very well Amelia could be hiding, waiting for the perfect moment to pounce.

Leave, his inner conscience pleaded. *Leave and let a group of active police officers deal with it. This isn't your job anymore.*

James shook his head, clearing the voices that wanted him to take the coward's way out of this situation. "I'm coming in!" he shouted to the mine, more for the words to propel his legs forward. He drew his gun and cocked it before starting into the mine, turning on the flashlight on his cell phone in the other hand. "Identify yourself if you're in there, or risk being shot."

Again, only his own echo replied. He reached the opening and turned his body sideways to slide in and avoid getting scratched by the splintered wood. He first directed the flashlight straight ahead, saw nothing, then pointed it to the ground.

"Fuck," he whispered, jumping back as he saw at least a dozen animal carcasses scattered about the ground, squirrels mostly, and a raccoon and rabbit, by the looks of them. The odor of death attacked his senses immediately, his eyes welling with tears as he buried his nose inside his elbow.

He took five seconds to gather himself, feeling a sudden urgency and flash of panic. It had become obvious that Amelia Doss was back in Ridgeway and had returned to haunt her old hiding spot. She wasn't here at the moment, but would return at some point. And if she wasn't here, then where was she? Strolling through town? Sitting down for a meal at the Elkhorn Diner?

James turned around, not needing to see any more, and bolted out of the mine. He gasped for fresh air once outside; the woods spinning around him as his head became light. He pulled out his cell phone and dialed Tyler's number, then quickly hung up.

"No. I'm not jumping to conclusions. No need to scare the kid. Not yet."

He left the mine behind and started his hike back down the mountain, not wasting a moment to get back to his truck as quickly as possible. He wouldn't so much as look at the Doss graves as he passed them by, and returned home to collect his thoughts and attempt to make sense of what he had just seen.

❦ 9 ❦

Tyler's wife, Avery, was an attractive blond with emerald-green eyes. She was home alone with the children and their annoying dog, which had been brought over by Tyler's mother the morning after Amelia moved into the walls. Amelia had never liked dogs, and the feeling appeared to be mutual. Even though she and Azazoth had kept to the shadows, dark corners, and the attic, the creature could sense them and kept running throughout the house, growling and barking.

"What the hell has gotten into you?" Avery kept asking the animal, bewildered by its odd behavior. "Perhaps we *do* have mice." She frowned and resumed unpacking boxes while the children played. Meanwhile, Azazoth drew the creature away while Amelia slid into the dark pantry, where Avery unpacked a collection of canned goods from a box she'd brought home the day before.

Amelia was, literally, inches from the woman, but Avery didn't seem to notice or sense her. It was curious that children and the mentally ill could see the shadows, and Amelia in her current ethereal form, but that most adults, for whatever reason, saw nothing. She contemplated this odd revelation for a few moments, catching herself watching Avery methodically place one can after another onto the shelves until the box was empty.

"Guess we're good on canned goods for a while," the woman muttered, as if she couldn't believe she had done all of her task. Only half the shelf was full. Avery strode from the pantry and went to work emptying the remaining shelf of stable groceries from another box. These she placed in a cupboard next to the refrigerator.

The dog must have been bored with Azazoth, because it came into the kitchen and settled on the mat in front of the sink.

"See? You've gone and tired yourself out. Now you're going to take a nap in the middle of the room I'm working in." Avery let out a resigned sigh, paused, and with her hands on her hips, surveyed the kitchen.

The dog stood suddenly, its eyes trained on the open pantry door. A low growl emerged from its throat and it trotted to the pantry entrance and began barking.

Amelia hissed like a cornered cat, then rushed the pantry door, causing the dog to yelp and retreat. She materialized, grabbed the door handle, and slammed the pantry door shut.

A bloodcurdling scream sounded from the kitchen, causing Amelia to pause. Had Avery seen her? She giggled and faded into the darkness, slinking back into the walls and up to the attic. At least in this room, the dog was less likely to bother them.

The attic was warm and dark, a few beams of afternoon sunlight streaming through the vents at both ends. She found Azazoth already there, lounging in a dark corner.

"We have to rid ourselves of that creature," Amelia said, imagining how good the animal flesh would taste, though blood more than flesh tasted better to her now. She remembered when eyeballs had been her favorite delicacy.

"We can strangle it. Leave it somewhere, so they can find it," Azazoth suggested.

"I don't care how we do it, just that we do. It's kind of hard to live in this house with a beast that constantly gives away our presence." She pursed her nonexistent lips together. Outside, a car door slammed shut, the dog below went nuts, there were footfalls, and then the door opened.

"Avery? What's wrong? You're white as a sheet." The voice was Tyler's.

Amelia straightened, exchanged a glance with Azazoth, then dove into the wall and slipped downstairs to find out what Avery had seen.

Tyler had his hands on Avery's shoulders, looking into her eyes.

The woman shuddered. "There was someone in the pantry. Buster growled at them and they rushed past him and slammed the pantry door shut. So," she paused, stifling a panicked sob, "I grabbed a knife and opened the pantry door and there was no one there." Tears began streaming down Avery's cheeks.

He just stood there, staring at her. Finally, he asked, "What did they look like?"

She shrugged. "I don't know. Like a shadow and a bony hand, but I could see through it." Avery drew in a ragged breath. "I think the house is haunted."

Tyler bit his lower lip.

"Come on, Ty! Do you realize I came down in the middle of the night last night and found all the chairs pulled out from the dining room table? That's not how we left them." Then she lowered her voice to a whisper. "The eyes I saw outside the window? The kids talking about the little girl in their closet? And now this..."

A deep furrow appeared in Tyler's brow as he frowned. He started toward the kitchen with Avery close behind. "And you didn't leave the kitchen to where someone could have run out?"

Amelia followed them.

"No. I didn't leave. No one could have gotten in *or* out."

Tyler inspected the pantry from top to bottom, as if he didn't believe her. "Son of a bitch," he muttered.

"What are we going to do?"

He looked at his wife. "Let's try to look at this logically…"

"Damn it, Ty! How logical is any of this? Go ahead—explain it to me. I'll wait."

Amelia smiled from her hiding place.

"I can't explain it. But we haven't been getting a lot of sleep. The kids and the move are likely stressing you out…"

"Great. I'm just stressed. Fine, but if one more thing happens, I'm taking the kids and going to your mom's until *you* sort it out." She jabbed a finger in his direction.

He threw up his hands. "What the hell can *I* do to sort it out?"

"I don't know, get a priest or something."

Amelia withdrew momentarily. A priest? She didn't like the sound of that.

"Fine. Maybe Danny has some ideas there."

"Why Danny?"

"The Amelia Doss incident," he said, as if that explained everything.

Apparently it did, because she nodded. "Well, it's doubtful this is *that* serious, but what is the likelihood we'd end up with a haunted house?"

"It's my luck," Tyler said, closing the pantry door. The look on his face hinted at disbelief.

"So, what did Jim Abbott want?"

Amelia perked up at the mention of Sheriff Abbott. She hadn't seen him in some time.

"Nothing. Just our monthly lunch."

"That's nice."

"Have you been letting the kids watch cartoons all afternoon?" Tyler started into the living room.

Avery followed with one last wary glance at the pantry door. "It's the only way I can get anything done. But maybe now that you're home, I can take a break and entertain the kids while *you* unpack some boxes we still haven't gotten to. Like the linen closet."

"Fair enough," he said.

The dog leapt against the wall Amelia was in and began scratching at it.

She glowered at the beast. If she could just lure it into a confined space, she could materialize and then kill it. Her attention shifted to the basement. There was nothing worthwhile down there except the furnace and water heater. Right now, it was serving as storage for holiday ornaments and other boxes full of things they wanted to keep, but didn't need day-to-day.

Amelia slid up the wall and over to the basement door. Once on the other side, she opened the door. The dog followed, its slick brown fur bristling. It was some kind of long, small dog. A breed Amelia had never seen before that seemed useless for home security. She closed the door behind it, then dove down the stairs, luring the animal down into a far corner. Once there, she materialized, reached down, and picked up all fifteen pounds of snarling teeth by the neck. The thing's teeth didn't hurt her one bit. How could they? With as much ease as breaking a twig, she snapped its little neck. It let out a single yelp just before she did it, probably because it knew it couldn't win against Amelia. She cocked her head to one side, looking at the dog hanging listlessly in her hand. Azazoth materialized from the darkness of the furnace room, four other shadows at his side. Funny how they always showed up when it was time to eat, even though it was usually Amelia catching the prey.

She got the first bite, though. Tearing into the dog's throat, she suckled its blood, quickly deciding she preferred wild rabbit. When she finished, she dropped the animal to the floor. The meat was soon covered in shadows, but Amelia didn't stick around to find out who was eating what. She retreated into the walls and upstairs to watch Tyler and Avery, and the children, Wyatt and Charlotte.

Amelia wasn't sure why she hadn't killed Tyler already. Perhaps it was interesting to watch the living, blissfully unaware of the world of shadows around them, go about their meaningless lives, pretending it all meant something. There were several opportunities to easily off him, but none of them had felt like the right time. "Patience," she whispered to herself.

Tyler stopped emptying the box of kitchen linens and looked around the room as if he'd heard something.

Amelia perked up. Could he hear her? "Tyler..." she whispered.

His brow furrowed and he looked around. Then he shook his head like he didn't want to believe it and went back to unloading the box.

She floated down from the ceiling to the kitchen table and pulled out a chair. Tyler's back had been turned, but he spun around to inspect the noise, his eyes widening when he saw the chair there. Amelia went to the second of four chairs and pulled it out while he watched it move all by itself. Then he bent his head over, closed his eyes and rubbed them. She put the chairs back. So, when Tyler opened his eyes again— the chairs stood where they were supposed to be.

"I'm finally fucking losing it," he muttered to himself. His eyes traveled the entire room. "Who's here?"

There was no response. Amelia could have easily replied, but there was no point. It was *much* more fun to watch him and his family lose their minds. Slowly. She fought back a cackle.

He looked around the room once more, then turned off the light and retreated to the living room, where Avery and the children were half-asleep on the couch. He sat in a reclining chair and leaned back.

"Sleep, my darlings," Amelia said, her voice dripping with vitriol. She watched over them while they restlessly snoozed.

The family never made it upstairs that night. Instead, they slept soundly in the living room, the television on in the background, the inaudible sound of cartoon characters sifting through the air. It wasn't until the children and Avery awoke the next morning that Tyler even stirred. As the rest of his family started their day, he slept until Wyatt gently prodded him. "Daddy, pancakes."

He mumbled something, then fully woke up. "What time is it?"

"Breakfast time," Wyatt said.

"Honey, have you seen Buster?" Avery came into the living room, still dressed in her sweats from the day before.

"No. He's probably upstairs, enjoying our bed all to himself," he said with a laugh.

If you only knew, Amelia thought, giggling softly to herself inside the wall. This was only the beginning.

❧ 10 ❧

Tyler slipped into their home office while Avery gave Charlotte a bath and Wyatt spent an hour in his room for reading practice. The morning had passed without issue, and Tyler accepted that perhaps he really was losing his mind.

He had thought he heard Amelia's voice whispering to him, but chalked it up as impossible. A quick phone call to Danny would help set him straight, or so he hoped. He dialed his friend and sat in the chair behind the desk.

"Hey, Ty, long time no talk. How have you been?" Danny greeted.

"Hey, Dan, I've been okay. How is the writing going?"

"No complaints. Going as well as I could hope."

"I've heard the rumors about your first book being picked up for a movie deal. That's pretty exciting."

"Yeah, sometimes it doesn't feel real, and I need to pinch myself. It's an insane process—can take years for anything to actually happen—but I suppose a foot is in the door with a major Hollywood studio."

"Congrats, man, we're all so proud of you. Are you even in town right now?"

Danny had a schedule that took him out of Ridgeway often. He'd travel to New York to meet with his publisher, stop at random cities for book signings, and now had regular flights to Hollywood for film discussions.

"I'm here. Actually, don't have anywhere to go for the next three weeks. Almost feels like a vacation, if I didn't have to meet my daily word count."

"That's great. We'll have to get together and catch up on life."

"Is something wrong, Ty? I can hear it in your voice."

Tyler looked around, ensuring he was not being listened to, and whispered into the phone. "I think she's back."

"What makes you say that?" Danny asked, his tone shifting to one of concern.

"There have been weird things going on around the house. Sounds from the walls, things being moved."

"Well, that could be something else, not necessarily . . . her."

They avoided speaking her name whenever possible, not wanting to contribute to the world's belief in Amelia Doss.

"I know, and that's why I called. You're more into this paranormal shit than I am. Can you think of anything it might be? We're the first owners of a brand-new house, so it can't be haunted, right?"

"Not likely, but not impossible, either. I mean, what existed on the land before? Have you seen anything with lights flickering? TVs turning themselves on or off?"

"Nothing like that."

"Hmm, paranormal activity usually interferes with electronics, so it might not be that, either."

"I don't know what to do. Think you might be able to come look around?"

"I can swing by within the next week. I'm pretty busy right now trying to meet a deadline for my editor."

Tyler didn't have a week to wait—he needed answers today. "Okay, that's fine. Maybe we'll plan for that dinner when you come—just let me know."

"Deal."

"Danny? Do you think she would come back to Ridgeway?"

Silence filled the airwaves for a few seconds, and Tyler checked his phone to make sure the call was still connected.

"If I didn't succeed in putting her back in the grave last time, then I suppose she would," Danny finally said. "She *has* to, Ty. No matter what happens, all roads lead back to Ridgeway. I mean, *if* she's back at all. It's a big *if*. If that's the case, and if we are to finish her off once and for all, we would need to get her by her grave. Because if she's back, she's not done hunting you down."

"That's a lot of ifs," Tyler said, knowing it wasn't a matter of *if*. It was *when*.

"Yes, it is," Danny said, his voice filled with uncertainty.

Tyler knew Danny didn't believe she was gone for good, either. "If she is back, then what is she waiting for? It's been fifteen years since our last encounter. I still think about it every day, waiting for her to show up."

"I think that's your answer, Ty. If she's back, she knows her failures from the past. She knows you're ready for her. Maybe she's waiting for when you won't be expecting it. She proved in college that she had no issue playing the long game, even toying with you for the fun of it. You won't be so lucky this time around—she'll want blood as quickly as she can get it."

"Then what can I do?"

"What you've been doing. I'm afraid the rest of your life might be this way. Unless she reveals she's back in Ridgeway, then we can look at some options for getting her back into her grave. I've never stopped researching. I have some things worth trying out that I think will work if the ritual fifteen years ago didn't."

"Well, I can't wait that long, Dan. I need something to happen right now."

"Stay patient. Time is all we need. If she really is here, then every day she lets pass is another day we gain an advantage. I'm sitting on a pile of gold in terms of information we can use to combat her."

Danny had never sounded so sure of himself. Tyler wanted to ask him to move in with the family, just to have his friend as an invaluable asset, in case Amelia showed up one random night. He knew she was getting closer. Stronger. But had no proof or way to convey his gut feeling.

"Okay, I'll trust you, Dan. Stay by your phone at all times, please." Tyler didn't know how else to convey the urgency of his worry. "I need to go around the neighborhood and find our dog—pretty sure he slipped out of the yard."

"Okay, we'll talk soon. Try to relax, Ty. No reason to suspect something is suddenly going on after all this time."

They hung up and Tyler drew a deep breath, letting it out in a long sigh. He slipped into his tennis shoes and went back downstairs. He crossed through the kitchen and stepped out the backdoor, quickly scanning the yard for any signs of the dog.

"Buster!" Tyler called out, his hands cupped around his mouth. "Here, boy!"

He whistled and waited, the neighborhood fortunately silent as he craned his neck to listen for the distant sound of Buster's jingling bell attached to his collar.

"Buster!"

The dog never came, so Tyler climbed down the porch and investigated around the yard. They had one gap where the dog might have been able to slip through, a fence picket that had eroded away after the last snowstorm. Tyler had moved a stack of bricks in front of the opening and was pleased to find them untouched. Buster had no way out of the backyard, and he confirmed this after walking along the entire perimeter, checking the fence and gate for any other potential openings.

Buster had a doghouse that contained his food and water bowls. Tyler checked there last, squatting down to look inside and finding nothing but an empty food bowl and half-full water bowl.

"What the fuck?" he whispered to himself, standing up and storming back to the house. "Buster!" he shouted one more time, knowing it didn't make a difference.

Tyler returned inside, discouraged and confused. He tried to slow his mind and think back to the sequence of events when he had last seen Buster. Avery had mentioned Buster was barking in the pantry, an odd event because the dog never went inside the pantry. They had been fortunate to have a dog not tear apart their furniture or any food he had easy access to.

Tyler pulled open the pantry door to double-check, finding nothing but cereal boxes, canned vegetables, and packages of pasta staring back.

He could have come back in and been locked in a room by accident.

Buster had occasionally hidden under the couch or the kids' beds. Tyler ran with this hope and checked under the couch. No dog. He raced up the stairs where Avery had just stepped out of the bathroom with Charlotte bundled up in towels after her bath.

"Everything okay?" she asked, eyebrows cocked in his direction.

"Yeah, just looking for Buster. I didn't see any way he

could have escaped from the backyard—he might just be hiding in the house somewhere."

"Oh, good. I'm sure he's around here somewhere. Say, could you grab me a new bottle of lotion from the basement for Charlotte? The one we have up here is all empty."

"Sure thing."

"They're in the box next to the laundry area—can't miss it."

"Okay, I'll be right back."

Tyler took a quick peek into the kids' bedrooms, checking under their beds, before heading back downstairs with his shoulders slumped and head hanging low. He crossed the living room and opened the door to the basement, flicking on the light that revealed the bare stairs and concrete walls below. Their basement served as an ongoing house project they chipped away every few weekends. Tyler planned to use his summer break to make a serious dent, now that they knew how they wanted to finish the basement. Until then, they only used the space for storage and laundry.

Tyler descended the stairs, brushing his hand along the wall since they didn't have a handrail installed yet. When he reached the bottom, the familiar musty smell filled his nose, as it would until they put drywall up and divided the laundry room from the rest of the basement.

"Baby lotion," he said, crossing the space and weaving through the maze of boxes toward the washer and dryer. The light dimmed the further he walked from the stairwell, the lone light in the basement positioned in the center of the room.

A box stood atop more boxes, its flaps opened, light yellow bottles of the baby lotion sticking out of the top. Tyler nodded as he reached in and grabbed one, reading the label to confirm he was getting the right item. Satisfied, he pivoted around and froze, noticing a trail of bloody footsteps along the path he had just walked.

"What the—?" he said, looking down to his feet. Blood smeared around the edges, so he raised his foot to see the sole, gasping when he saw it completely drenched in blood. He put his foot down, blood squirting from the edges of his shoe and creating another bloody footprint on the concrete floor.

His heart immediately started drumming, pounding in his ears as he scanned the basement for the source of the blood. Tyler followed the trail of footprints, leading him nearly back to the bottom of the stairwell. The towers of boxes had formed a fort in this area, mostly old college textbooks and little decorations for the basement.

The dark crimson liquid spread out from the base of these boxes, and Tyler was grateful to not have slipped and fallen on his initial pass through. He stood on his tiptoes to see over the top box, but it proved ineffective. Instead, he moved the top couple of boxes from each stack, setting them beside him in a mindless effort as his eyes remained focus on what lay behind them. For a split second, he thought something had leaked out of one of these old boxes, but the way things had been going, he knew it had to be blood.

"Oh my God!" he cried, dropping the last box he had grabbed. Behind the boxes lay Buster, in the middle of the bloody pool, his body limp, his tongue hanging out of his mouth like a dead fish.

Tyler's hands shot up to his mouth as the urge to vomit swelled within his stomach and throat. He couldn't look away, Buster's lifeless eyes staring to the ceiling. His legs locked, and he couldn't move away, either.

"Avery!" he shouted up the stairs as loud as he could. "You need to come down here right now!" A bead of sweat trickled down his face, despite the basement being the coolest room in the house. He waited as Avery's footsteps rumbled from above, trying to think of an explanation that didn't involve Amelia.

But he knew better. This had every sign of her handiwork.

Amelia Doss is back.

❧   I I   ❧

It was starting all over again. Danny knew it; he could feel it in his bones. Somehow, Amelia Doss was back. But how could he prove it, and how were they going to finally get rid of her? He'd lied to Tyler about having a new plan. Well, partially. Twice now, the rituals he'd tried had only put her back into the grave temporarily. The last one for fifteen years. Tyler knew she was back, too. Danny, however, wanted to deny it. He wanted to find a different explanation. Paranoia, perhaps? PTSD could do that to a person. He hoped it was all just a crazy coincidence and that his instincts were wrong.

"Some really eerie stuff has been happening at the house," Tyler had started the strange conversation.

As Danny had listened, he took notes. Now he looked down at the pad of paper and read over them. Chairs moving by themselves. Muffled voices and whispers. A little girl named Alice in the kids' bedroom closet, along with a shadow monster with sharp teeth and red eyes. The hand Avery had seen shut the pantry door, and the missing dog. "Probably dead," Danny muttered to himself.

This wasn't Amelia's method, though, which made it all the weirder. Then again, Amelia had abandoned her MO back in Denver fifteen years ago. What Tyler had going on at the house seemed like classic poltergeist activity, minus the typical electrical interference. Danny left the notepad on the kitchen table and went into his office. His eyes scanned the bookshelves for the occult books he'd bought all those years ago. Along with them, he knew he'd find the notebook with his old notes. Down in the far-left corner of the largest bookcase, he spotted them. He leaned down and pulled them out and blew off the dust. He hadn't looked at these in years. Ever since he'd given up becoming a screenwriter, after more rejections than he cared to admit, the story of Amelia Doss lost its appeal as a subject anyone would want to watch a movie about, let alone a book. With a heavy sigh, he brought the books and the notebook back to his desk and sat down. Putting on his reading glasses, he began flipping through the notebook. Where should he start? Was the display at the museum enough to have kept her going all these years? Surely, they would have seen signs of Amelia before now.

Then again, Tyler had just moved back to Ridgeway, and because it was Tyler's ancestor who'd killed her, it could have been his presence that brought her back. But why? He flipped to the last page. There was nothing not already burned into his memory. Danny sat back in the chair. "I need to look at this rationally," he said aloud to the empty room. "First, there's no reason to believe she's back. Second, maybe Tyler's house really is haunted. Strange for a new development, but there are unmarked graves all over this area. Lots of settlers died here during the Gold Rush," he told himself.

The doorbell rang, and Danny practically jumped out of his skin. He glanced at the clock. It was already eight, and he wasn't expecting anyone. The doorbell rang again. He got up and went to the door, peering through the peephole first, only to find James Abbott standing on his front porch. While Danny had been back in Ridgeway longer than Tyler, he rarely talked to the old sheriff. They would nod at one another if they passed on the street, but they weren't buddies by any means. Danny opened the door. "Mr. Abbott?"

"Danny. Do you mind if I come in for a moment? I have something I need to get off my mind and you're the only person I can talk to." The retired sheriff's face was grim.

He stood to the side and opened the door. "Sure." Inside, his stomach twisted and an icy chill ran the length of his body, turning his bare arms to gooseflesh.

James looked around. "Nice place. How long have you been back now?"

"About nine years," he said. "You want a beer?"

"That would be nice. Yeah." James walked across the living room to a table of plants and pictures near the window.

Danny's mother had given him the plants to liven up the place, and Danny was convinced they thrived on neglect. He only watered them when he remembered, maybe two or three times a month. A house sitter did it in his absence. But despite this, they survived. He disappeared into the kitchen and returned with two bottles, caps off, and handed one to James. "Have a seat."

James nodded and sat.

Danny sat across from him. "So, what's on your mind?"

"You write all those horror novels," James said.

"Not really police procedurals or anything, but FBI agents, amateur detectives, or laymen who get caught up in a terrifying mystery," Danny said, wondering when James was going to get to the point. The former sheriff hadn't aged too much. His face appeared more weathered, his eyes tired, but his expressions and mannerisms hadn't changed. It also appeared he'd kept himself fit, even in retirement.

"Amelia Doss," James started. Danny's stomach lurched,

and he swallowed. "Do you think it would be crazy if I told you I was worried she might be back?"

"Why would you think that?" *First Tyler, now the sheriff,* Danny's mind screamed.

"Just a hunch. Instinct, you know? But I certainly don't want to tell Tyler. Can't believe he's married with a couple of kids." He motioned to Danny. "Even you, with your big career. You kids make me feel old." He took a swig of the beer, his gaze toward the window. But James wasn't looking at anything specific. He appeared to be looking beyond the window, into the past.

Danny decided it might not be wise to share what Tyler had told him. It wasn't his place, and he didn't want James to worry. It might give him a heart attack or something, though the former sheriff wasn't quite seventy. Hell, he didn't know exactly how old James Abbott was, but it was certainly fifteen years older than he had been since the last time Amelia Doss showed up. "What *kind* of hunch?" Danny pressed.

"A couple times a week, I head up to the old mine. Check out the gravesite—just in case she comes back. I never see anything. But this last time I found the mine had been broken into and a few dead animals. The grave looks like it's been disturbed. Like it's developed a strange hole..." James' voice trailed off.

Danny shuddered, but washed the feeling away with a deep gulp of his beer, hoping the alcohol would numb that growing dread in his gut. "We could have a mountain lion."

The sheriff nodded. They both knew it wasn't a mountain lion. Besides, mountain lions weren't common in Ridgeway. Ten years earlier, a coyote had been caught taking dogs and cats out of people's yards. "Could be a coyote or a fox? Just the state of the animals. Predators eat a lot more."

He suddenly found himself trying to deny it with logical

explanations. "Unless the predator was chased off. Or maybe a bird of prey. Lots of owls and hawks here."

"Mmm." James Abbott turned to him. "Don't you ever find it uncomfortable working in the Ridgeway Museum with the picture of her staring you down like that?"

"As far as I'm concerned, Amelia Doss is ancient history. I did that ritual..."

"You're right. I'm probably being paranoid. Hazard of living the job for so many years. That was the only cold case left open when I retired. It still vexes me to this day." James took another drink of his beer. "Will you do me a favor, though?"

"Anything," Danny said, regretting it as soon as it left his lips.

"If you see any signs, you'll let me know, right?"

Danny nodded. "Of course."

"And don't say anything to Tyler. I know you went through a lot, too, and don't think I'm trying to make your experience trivial when I say this, but Tyler has been through a *lot*." He shook his head. "No reason to bring up terrible memories unless absolutely necessary."

"I agree," Danny said.

James finished his beer and set the empty bottle on a piece of paper on the coffee table. "I should get going. Didn't mean to drop by unannounced. Just had to tell someone, you know?"

Danny stood, nodding numbly. "I'll definitely keep my eyes open. Anytime you need someone to talk to..."

"Thanks, kid. You and Tyler, I always liked you two. Thought you were snot-nosed hoodlums when I first met you, but I was wrong about that. You're good people." He reached out to shake Danny's hand.

Danny obliged, then opened the door. "Take care, Mr. Abbott."

"Jim," James corrected. "I think we've been through enough together to warrant first name familiarity." Jim tipped his head. "Have a good night."

"You, too, Jim," Danny said, not liking how it sounded. It felt almost too familiar, even disrespectful. Calling him "Mister" was strange enough.

The former Ridgeway sheriff returned to his truck, and Danny closed the door, locking it. He stood there for a minute, then shook the feeling off. He needed to concentrate on Tyler and his haunted house problem. If Amelia turned out to be the cause, which was unlikely, they would deal with it then. In the meantime, he was going to have to do some research on ghosts, hauntings, and poltergeist activity.

If Danny was nothing else, he prided himself on being an excellent researcher. He cleared away the empty beer bottles and started a pot of coffee in the kitchen, then grabbed his notepad, a pen, and his laptop, and made himself comfortable in the living room. With a fresh cup of coffee in hand, he began looking up hauntings. When his cup was empty, he glanced at the clock, realizing it was already eleven. But he'd gotten some good information already. Every phenomenon Tyler had told him about mimicked a classic haunting with poltergeist activity. It was also quite possible the dog had run away, since several of the cases Danny had found mentioned runaway pets. Spirits often didn't like animals and would try to chase them off. However, the only way they were going to find out who or what was haunting the house would be by digging into that parcel of land in the historical records. Even then, if a random person had been buried there, there may not have been any records at all.

The other option was to call his old friend Lavinia, who ran the Denver occult shop, *Dark Works*. Danny called her from time to time to talk and had attended some of her workshops for witches over the years. Her whole belief system and lifestyle inspired him, and he'd even written a book where the main character was helped by a witch. He'd based the character on Lavinia. Their friendship was platonic; she was a good ten years older. He'd thought about it, of course. But beyond his interest in the dark arts and her lifestyle, he was sure they had little else in common. Now he wanted to call her and unload all this craziness into her lap. She had a way of easing his fears and explaining the supernatural in ways that made sense. Lavinia also made the supernatural and magic feel practical and useful. He knew she would know exactly what to do in Tyler's situation. If that meant finding a medium to talk to the spirit and get rid of it, then so be it. But right now, it was too late to bother her.

Stretching his arms, he stifled a yawn. Closing the laptop, he set it back on the coffee table, picked up his mug, and went to the kitchen to rinse it out. Then he turned off the coffeepot and the lights, leaving a small lamp in the living room on like he always did. It made him feel safer knowing that people might think he was awake if they saw a light on. It was only after he checked all the doors and windows were locked for the second time that he went to bed, wondering if maybe Tyler had something about him that attracted supernatural phenomena. Once he decided to research that at the library in the morning, he fell asleep quickly.

He dreamt he stood in a black room, so dark that the lightless murk seemed to writhe around him. His feet were anchored to the floor with an invisible weight. He screamed, but the darkness swallowed all sound.

Chad Gunther was a typical outdoorsy Colorado-type. Originally from Boulder, he moved to Ridgeway because it was the trendy thing to do. If you could afford it, of course. He had a high-tech work-from-home job, ran five miles every day, loved to ski, canoe, hike, and bike. Chad had never found the right woman, and didn't like the idea of being tied down and worrying about anyone but himself. He was vain, liked craft beer, and knew more useless facts than most people. Being a know-it-all was something he prided himself on. Unfortunately, one thing he didn't know about were the shadows inside his walls, writhing around in the darkness, watching his every move. To them, he was merely fresh meat.

AZAZOTH AND AMELIA SAT IN THE ATTIC RAFTERS OF THE Reynolds house in silence. Amelia was thinking about her next move, and Azazoth was watching her intently, as if hanging onto her every thought. Other shadows came and went, slipping through the dark places and whispering as they passed. Amelia paid them no attention at first, until one of them glided by her whispering, "Kill Chad."

She lifted a semi-opaque eyebrow, a sly grin sliding over her lips. Azazoth smiled in response. She stopped the passing shadow with, "Who's Chad?"

The thing cackled then growled, "The neighbor."

Azazoth turned giddy. "Yes, let's kill the neighbor."

She found sitting in the attic all day boring, but it had to be the right time. Killing Tyler was a task she wanted to savor. Scaring him and his family was enjoyable, but it would only be a matter of time before she grew bored with that and would kill Tyler in haste. No, his had to be a long, suffering death. She wanted him terrified, yet she found it all exhausting, and a fresh life source to feed her weary form sounded like a much-needed diversion. For a few hours, at least.

The lone shadow hovered next to her, its expectant eyes watching her with curiosity.

"Where is this Chad?" she asked.

"Follow me," the shadow said, slipping through the attic to the vent and out. Amelia and Azazoth followed, keeping to the deep shade of late afternoon. They squirmed to the ground, like worms in the dirt, and burrowed their way beneath the fence separating the houses onto a fully shaded, covered porch in the backyard. The unnamed shadow dove straight into a dark window well and into the basement. Again, Amelia and Azazoth followed, slipping into the walls, making their way to the dining room where Chad sat polishing his skis. With each minute that passed, the sun settled further behind the Rocky Mountains, leaving the house dark except for a small lamp.

By Amelia's estimation, Chad was about six-foot-two, a strong one-hundred and seventy-five pounds, and in his mid-to-late thirties. His brown hair was unkempt and longer than most men of this time kept it, settling right at his shoulders. A strange buzz emanated from the cellular phone on the side table next to him.

Chad picked it up. "Brian, bro!" Then he listened, a huge smile slipping over his too-thin lips. "Yeah, man! That would be sweet! Would love to explore the caves!"

"Caves?" Azazoth perked up.

Amelia rolled her eyes. "We'll kill him long before he makes it to any caves," Amelia told him.

Azazoth gave her a look telling her she'd spoiled his fun. There would be plenty of time for caves later. But she didn't tell him that.

Chad frowned. "Dude, hold on a minute." He took the phone from his ear and cocked his head, as if he'd heard something.

"He can hear us," Amelia whispered.

"Good," Azazoth said.

"All he hears are the whispers," the unknown shadow said with a squeal of delight.

Amelia giggled.

"What the fuck?" Chad stood up and brought the phone back to his ear. "Dude, let me call you back. It sounds like someone's in my house." A long pause ensued as he listened to whoever was on the other end of the conversation. "No, I don't think I need the cops. Sounds like little kids. I thought I heard a little girl giggle. Could be from outside, but it almost sounded like it was inside." Another pause. "The new neighbors next door have two little kids. Annoying, loud little shits."

Chad went over to the front room window and peered out toward Tyler's house. "Yeah, probably the neighbors," he said. "Tell you what, call me tomorrow with the details. I'm totally game for that. Catch you later, bro!" He tapped the screen, drew in a deep breath, and looked around. Finally, he shook his head and returned to his chair, polishing his skis.

Upon closer inspection, Amelia saw he was waxing them. "Why would one put wax on skis?" she asked the shadows.

Both Azazoth and the unnamed shadow merely shrugged. Not being from the physical realm, it was doubtful they knew why humans did anything.

Amelia assessed the situation from directly behind Chad's chair, only inches from his head. She could have easily snapped his neck and been done with it. She didn't see Azazoth dodge into the kitchen and return with the cleaver until he held it out to her.

Chad must have seen it from the corner of his eye, because he jumped up and backed away.

Her eyes widened in surprise. Did he merely see a meat cleaver floating in the air, or did he see them, too?

"What the hell?!" He made a run for the front door, but Azazoth materialized and barred his way, hovering in the air in front of Chad, fangs and red eyes gleaming.

Amelia materialized, too. "Chad," she said.

He opened his mouth to scream, but as he did, the unnamed shadow dove into the man's mouth, and all that emerged was a stifled, choking sound.

Azazoth moved in and shapeshifted, wrapping himself around Chad like a snake.

"Very good, my friends," Amelia said. She approached the bound and gagged man, his eyes wide with horror. "My name is Amelia Doss."

Chad struggled even harder. He knew who she was. She could feel the belief emanating from him in waves of terror.

She stepped up beside him, put the cleaver to his throat, pulled back, and swung. It only went in a quarter inch. "Unfortunately for you, your cleaver is dull," she said.

His eyes rolled back into his head as she hacked at his

neck, blood spurting in all directions from the blows, until finally she hit the spinal column. It took a few more whacks before she had completely severed his head. When it finally toppled to the floor with a dull thud, Amelia dropped the cleaver and supped the blood from his neck. That's when she realized Chad's body was still standing. She looked down to find the shadows holding the body steady for her. Once she'd drank her fill, only then did they let the body drop.

"May the rest of us feast?" the unnamed shadow asked.

Amelia nodded, shifting from her physical form back into a shadow. She stood back and watched as her almost constant companions, shadows of all shapes and sizes, descended on the corpse to drink what was left of him.

Azazoth emerged from the bottom of the heap of shadows after a few minutes, his red eyes blazing with euphoria.

"We should get back," Amelia said, her attention shifting toward the Reynolds house next door.

"Should we place his body..." Azazoth started.

She didn't wait for him to finish. "Do as you wish." Then Amelia turned and drifted, like smoke, through the kitchen window, which was open just a crack, and made her way back into the attic next door. Still stunned by the sheer power of Chad's fear and how it fed her, she devised a new plan. Since she still had to eat, she had no choice but to kill, which would alert Tyler to her presence. Unless she did it carefully.

Eavesdropping on conversations was easy when one could lurk in a dark corner and listen. No one except the children could see her, and they'd finally been sent back to their own rooms, Amelia's presence was written off as a product of the children's imaginations. So she'd spent her time listening. Tyler worked at the high school. The same school he'd gone to years before. *There's plenty of food there,* she thought.

"You should follow him and choose your targets wisely," came Azazoth's voice from beside her.

She'd felt him enter the attic. "As I planned," she said.

"They will know you're back soon."

"They will." A sly grin slid onto her lips, and she turned to Azazoth. "What will they do about it? A ridiculous ritual that merely puts me to sleep for a few years before I come back? I *always* come back."

Azazoth snickered, but stopped short when the hatch to the attic opened and the stairs were drawn down.

"I keep hearing it up there," came Avery's voice.

"What kind of noise?" Tyler asked. Heavy steps ascended the ladder, and a light beamed into the darkness, sending both Amelia and Azazoth scurrying into the dark corners. He looked around.

"Maybe it's raccoons. Or mice. Or rats! Something killed the damn dog, Ty."

Tyler let out a heavy sigh. He began sweeping the flashlight slowly over every inch of the attic, leaving Amelia and Azazoth time to move back into the dark places where it was safe, and they'd remain unseen. "I don't see any insulation out of place."

"What do you mean?" his wife asked.

"If there were raccoons up here, they'd be ripping up the insulation. The same with mice or rats. I don't see any sign of creatures. No birds." He examined the rafters and roof more closely from where he stood. Then he turned and looked back down the ladder. "I don't see any mouse droppings or any place in the roof where something might have gotten in." Then his eyes and his light went to the vents. "The vents are sealed."

"So, you think I'm crazy?"

He chuckled. "Of course not. Beams and fittings can

expand and contract with the heat and cold. Houses settle, Avery."

"Fine, but what about the voices? It sounds like someone whispering up there."

Amelia smiled, even though no one would see it.

"Here..." Tyler climbed back down the ladder. "You go up and look yourself. There's no one up there."

"What about the chairs? The thing I saw in the pantry?"

There was an uncomfortable span of silence.

"Yes, Tyler. Explain that," Amelia whispered.

"See! There it is again."

"Go, look for yourself," Tyler said.

"I'm not going up there. It's ghosts."

Amelia held back the laughter threatening to erupt from her throat.

"Fine." Exasperation filled his voice.

The ladder came up, locked in place, and the attic hatch closed, leaving them to the darkness again.

Amelia moved closer, stretching her ear to the attic hatch so she could hear them better.

"Did you hear it?" Avery asked.

"I did." Tyler couldn't deny it. "But Danny researched the house and there was nothing."

"We need to get a priest in here or something."

"Maybe..." He let out a sigh. "It hasn't tried to hurt us yet."

"No, but it's scared the shit out of me and the kids." Her voice went low, almost threatening.

"The kids just have overactive imaginations. For all we know, it was the kids who moved the chairs. As for whatever you saw in the pantry—you were exhausted. I mean, have you seen it since?"

Amelia stuck her head into the wall and shoved her face through the ceiling so she could see them. Their fear of the unknown wasn't nearly as enjoyable when she couldn't witness it.

Avery crossed her arms over her chest. "No."

"All I'm saying is we should try to be practical until..."

"No, you're right." Avery lifted her hands in mock surrender. "Until I see something when I'm wide awake, I need to relax."

Tyler nodded. "Exactly." He pulled her into a hug, then withdrew and planted a kiss on her forehead. "That noise is probably a pipe or the air coming through the vents or something. We'll figure it out, eventually."

His wife nodded and gave him a weak smile. "I'm sure you're right." Then she glanced at her watch. "I suppose I should get the kids ready for bed."

Avery disappeared down the hallway and down the stairs, leaving Tyler alone in the hallway. He looked around. "If you're here, I'm going to find you, you bitch," he whispered, his eyes searching both ends of the hallway.

I sincerely hope so, Amelia thought, as she slipped back into the attic and out of sight.

❧ 13 ❧

The next morning, a Sunday, a knock banged on the front door just after Tyler had woken at eight o'clock to use the bathroom. The house remained still and silent.

Tyler peeked out his bedroom window and saw a police car parked along the sidewalk. His stomach immediately dropped. An officer knocking at the door on a Sunday morning could only mean one thing.

Danny popped into his mind first, but he dismissed it. His parents still lived in Ridgeway and would be the ones notified if something had happened to their son. In fact, the police didn't do this for anyone besides family. His palms slickened with sweat as he slipped on a robe and made his way down the stairs, the officer knocking once more. He had just seen his parents yesterday and everything was fine, so it had to be something else.

Tyler opened the front door and saw the familiar face of Sheriff Rachel Lloyd, James' deputy back when they were hunting down Amelia Doss all those years ago. She had won the first election after James' retirement and had already settled into her role as the town's new sheriff.

"Good morning, Mr. Reynolds," she greeted. Sheriff Lloyd wore her tan uniform and a matching cowboy hat, which she tipped upon seeing Tyler.

"Good morning?" Tyler asked, peering around the sheriff for clues to what might be going on. There were more police cars at the house next door.

"I'm sorry to bother you so early," she said. "But I'm afraid your neighbor was murdered yesterday."

Tyler's mouth dropped open, his mind racing in a million different directions.

"Chad? Murdered? How? Why?" Tyler caught himself speaking like a confused child, and forced his jaw back shut.

"We were hoping you might have some insight. When was the last time you saw him?"

Tyler pursed his lips and ran through his memory. "I think it was a couple days ago, saw him out working on his yard when I got home from work."

"And did you speak with him?"

"No, just waved, and he waved back. We didn't talk too much. My family's only been here a few months, and he keeps to himself."

"Have you seen any cars parked over there recently?"

"Not that I recall. I think it's his girlfriend that stops by from time to time. She drives a silver Nissan sedan."

"It was one of his friends who called us. They had a hike planned earlier this morning, and he didn't show up."

"Jesus," Tyler whispered, his hand moving toward his mouth. Amelia Doss quickly jumped to the forefront of his thoughts. She had shown similar patterns in the past, killing people within Tyler's circle, even he didn't know them on a personal basis. Chad fit the category perfectly, and he couldn't help but probe further.

"Can I ask . . . how?"

Sheriff Lloyd shifted uncomfortably from side to side, looking to the ground before meeting Tyler's eyes. "All I can say is that it was a violent, brutal attack."

They locked eyes, their history dancing in the space between them. Deputy Lloyd had been as much a part of the group trying to hunt down Amelia fifteen years ago, perhaps even more valuable than James Abbott because she actually believed in what had happened. The moment lingered, Tyler using subtle eye movements to beg the sheriff to confirm what he believed. What they all believed. But she said nothing on the matter.

"You all keep an eye out for anything out of the ordinary, and call me if you think of something that might be helpful. Stay safe, Mr. Reynolds." Rachel nodded to him and turned back down the walkway, returning to the house next door, where a team of detectives and forensics had just arrived.

Tyler remained in the doorway for another minute, watching the commotion unfold next door, feeling the gradual formation of a pit in his stomach.

This isn't happening, he thought. *There is a realistic explanation for what happened next door. Someone committed the murder. Someone who lives in this world with an actual, physical body. Someone who can stand trial and go to prison.*

As much as he tried to convince himself of these simple facts, doubt nudged within his mind, planting itself and demanding his full attention. He fought to keep Amelia Doss out of his thoughts, but he simply couldn't.

While it might be some time until the details came out, Tyler expected to hear of poor Chad being cut apart at the limbs, bite marks surely present to make the detectives wonder if an animal had somehow slipped into his home and killed him. They'd waste a day on that theory, but Tyler knew what it really meant.

He dialed Danny, but his friend didn't answer. Tyler needed to fill him in on these recent developments next door. The knocking apparently hadn't startled anyone in the house, as Tyler found it completely silent when he closed the door and bolted it shut.

"Okay, relax," he whispered to himself. "Just because it *could* be her, doesn't mean it is. It could be Chad's friend. Most murders are done by someone who knows the victim."

This only reassured him so much. While that logic could apply to this specific incident, it still didn't gel with the rest of the big picture. The sounds in the walls, the alleged appearance of monsters in the kids' closet, the dead dog. And now a dead neighbor. Tyler couldn't deny these as random coincidences, especially finding Buster in the basement.

Something bigger was at play, and it all centered around the Reynolds household. Tyler went to the garage and fished out the package of rat traps he had purchased last summer. All he could do was hold on to what little sense remained. The sounds in the walls and ceiling could be addressed with the traps. If the sounds continued and the traps remained empty, then they had a bigger problem on their hands. If they worked, then Tyler will have eliminated one issue, and would be ready to move on to the next matter.

He moved through the house, looking for the best places to put the three traps he had. He started in the basement, avoiding the area where he had found Buster, the blood since mopped away. Rats and mice preferred dark spots along the perimeter, so he dropped the first trap in the furthest corner of the basement, recognizing the stacks of boxes as the perfect hiding spot for a little rodent.

Tyler grabbed the next trap and returned upstairs, pleased to find the house still quiet as he maneuvered through it like a madman. He wanted a trap on every floor, so he placed one behind the living room couch. It would remain out of sight and reach from the kids and still get the job done.

He went upstairs, holding the last trap under his arm like a football, and decided on the attic. There had definitely been sounds coming from above them while they lay in bed at night, something he couldn't deny, like the closet monsters and supposed sounds within the walls. When he reached the upstairs landing, he paused for a moment as he stared at the drawstring hanging from the attic door above. He peered down the hallway, listening for any movement from the kids' room or his bedroom. The only sound upstairs belonged to Avery, snoring in a steady rhythm.

Tyler reached up and gripped the end of the drawstring, pulling it down with plenty of force, the door hinges creaking and moaning loud enough to bounce down the hallway. He braced himself for one of the kids to run out of their room, but neither of them came. Ready to get this over with, he pulled down the steps and climbed up, refusing to fully enter the attic, instead reaching above his head and positioning the trap right next to the door.

The last thing he wanted was to be alone in the attic. Just in case.

Right as he placed the trap and took his first step back down the stairs, his cell phone rang a loud, piercing chime that startled him and caused him to lose his footing and slide the rest of the way down, hitting the floor with a thud hard enough to wake the house.

"Fuck!" he muttered through gritted teeth, pain shooting from his ankles to his knees.

Avery's feet hit the floor, and she bolted out of the bedroom at the end of the hallway. "Ty, are you okay?!" she asked, appearing in the doorway, eyes bulging as they bounced from him to the open attic door. "What are you doing?"

"I'm fine, just fell on my way down. I was putting rat traps around the house, wanted one up in the attic."

"That's what you got out of bed for?" Avery asked, crossing her arms over her bosom and rubbing her arms.

"Well, no—"

"Mommy! Daddy!" Charlotte cried from her bedroom doorway, standing with a wide smile and a teddy bear wrapped in a hug.

"Good morning, sweetie," Avery said, opening her arms for Charlotte to run into. "Is your brother still sleeping?"

"Yeah."

"Something happened," Tyler said. "I'll have to tell you about it—in private. I need to call Danny back."

Tyler could only assume it was Danny who had called and caused his fall down the stairs. He checked his phone to confirm and dialed him back, his arms trembling as he wanted to avoid Avery and the kids from overhearing his conversation.

"Tyler?" Danny answered.

"Hey, Danny," Tyler said. "How are you?"

He tried to sound relaxed, not wanting to lead Avery on to anything suspicious. Fortunately, Charlotte grabbed Avery's hand and pulled her into her bedroom, Tyler shuffling into the office and closing the door.

"I'm okay," Danny replied. "Just thought I'd check in. Is something wrong? You sound out of breath."

"Sorry," Tyler whispered. "Had to step into the other room. Something happened here . . . well, next door."

"What's going on?"

"My neighbor was murdered. There are all kinds of cop cars outside. Sheriff Lloyd came to my door about a half hour ago and told me. Asked me if I'd seen anything in recent days."

"Shit. And she probably didn't mention if they have a suspect already, right?"

"Nope. That's why I'm worried. Our dog has been killed, and now our neighbor. What am I supposed to do? How am I not supposed to think of you-know-who?"

There was a long pause from Danny. Finally, he said, "We're headed into dangerous territory, Ty. Especially if the police come back with no suspects. I think we need to start meeting again—in person. Will you be able to do that?"

Getting away in the evenings had become a difficult task since the kids were born, Tyler not wanting to leave Avery to tend to them alone. But an unsettling reality had crept its way back into the lives of those in Ridgeway, even if they hadn't yet realized it. Tyler had no choice but to meet with Danny if he wanted any of chance of being around for his kids in the future. It was time to settle this matter once and for all.

"I can meet with you. Just let me know when."

James knocked on the front door, taking a step back to steal a glance next-door, where yellow tape remained around the property. All the vehicles and crime scene investigators had left for the day, sure to be back in the morning to wrap things up.

Rachel had called James shortly after he finished breakfast, informing him of the murder and seeking advice on how to best proceed. They chatted for fifteen minutes, James having pushed his most recent trip to the mine to the back of his thoughts. However, it all came crashing down when Rachel had mentioned the murder took place directly next door to Tyler Reynolds.

Tyler had invited James over for dinner several times since moving back to Ridgeway, but the ex-sheriff had declined, mainly because he didn't wait until six o'clock to eat dinner any more. By that time, he was used to being stuffed and usually slipped into his pajamas to watch game shows before calling it a night.

He had no plans of staying for dinner—he had already

eaten a fine Italian sandwich from Tony's Deli—and wanted to stop by to make sure Tyler was doing okay.

The doorknob jiggled before Tyler appeared, his face widening into a grin as soon as he saw James.

"Sheriff Abbott?" he asked. "What are you doing here?"

"C'mon, Reynolds, I told you to stop calling me the sheriff—that's Ms. Lloyd now. Which is exactly why I'm here. She called me this morning and told me about what happened next-door."

Tyler looked down at his feet as he shifted his weight from side to side. "Yeah. I'm still trying to come to terms with that. It's been a long day. Avery isn't doing too well—she's horrified that we live next door to such a scene."

"You're in a beautiful neighborhood—this is an outlier. Do you mind if I come in?"

"Yes, I'm so sorry, please do."

Tyler stepped aside and cleared the pathway for James to enter. He stepped in and slipped out of his shoes, looking around the house. He saw a stairwell leading upstairs, family pictures hanging on the walls. The clattering of pots and pans came from the kitchen around the corner, a little girl sitting on the couch with a coloring book splayed open across her lap.

"Is that Charlotte?" James asked, cocking his eyebrows.

"Sure is."

"My goodness, has it been that long? I don't think I've seen her since she was born."

Tyler shrugged. "I suppose it has been a while."

"Look, Reynolds, I don't want to take up your time, I just wanted to see how you're doing. I know with a murder taking place next door, you must be thinking about . . . her."

Tyler nodded, and James watched as his young friend fidgeted with his fingers.

Avery came around the corner and ran up to James, her

arms wide to embrace him. "Mr. Abbott," she said, one of the few people to have taken to heart his request to no longer be addressed as a sheriff. "It's so great to see you. Are you still enjoying retirement?"

They had spent time together in the weeks leading up to James' exhibit opening at the museum. Avery had volunteered to get matters organized for the unveiling ceremony, and worked with James to have it be just the way he wanted.

"You mean my new life as a professional golfer?" James replied with a chuckle. "I can't complain."

"Why don't you boys come sit in the kitchen? You don't have to stand here at the door."

"Thanks, babe," Tyler said. "But I was actually going to step outside to chat—it's about what happened next door. Don't want the kids to overhear anything."

"Okay, good idea. Can I get you a lemonade or anything, Mr. Abbott?" Avery asked.

"I'm okay, dear, thank you."

Avery offered a small grin before turning around and heading back to the kitchen.

"Shall we, then?" James asked, reaching for the front door behind him.

Tyler grabbed a small jacket and slipped into it before following James outside. He closed the door, pulling on it to make sure it wouldn't accidentally open.

"I'm happy for you, Reynolds," James said. "You have a beautiful little family. Glad you came back to Ridgeway."

"Thank you. I was glad, too, until recently. It's feeling like the same story unfolding. Do you sense that?"

"I don't know about all that. This is one murder. Back then, it seemed there was a new murder every day around here."

"So if there's another one tomorrow, then you'll suspect

something?" Tyler asked this with a slight tinge of resentment swimming behind his voice.

James understood his frustration and fear, and debated telling him what he came here to say—it might only make things worse for the already frazzled high-school teacher. "Don't be so optimistic, Reynolds, Jesus Christ. I'm on your side, remember?"

"Do you think Sheriff Lloyd is considering Amelia Doss?"

James had expected this question long before his arrival.

"She hasn't ruled it out, and that's all I can say on her behalf."

"Ruled it out," Tyler muttered under his breath, shaking his head. "You can't treat her like a normal suspect—it's so much more complicated than that."

James raised his hand. "Tyler, I need you to breathe. I understand you're disturbed by what happened. I know I would be, too. But it's not healthy or productive to jump to conclusions."

"I'm sorry, Sheriff—Mr. Abbott. It's hard for me to *not* assume it was Amelia."

"Well, you may not be wrong. I found something when I was last up at the mine."

"What?! You went? You were supposed to call me!"

James grinned. "As much as you may not like it, Reynolds, you are not my mother and I don't have to check in with you."

Tyler's jaw hung open. "Well, what did you find?"

James crossed his arms and stepped back another step, leaning on his back leg. "Dead animals inside the mine. Someone broke through the barrier. Granted, it wasn't the sturdiest job, but it was enough to require a concentrated effort to get inside."

"Shit. Did you explore any further inside?"

"Nope. I saw enough. The dead animals looked the same as the ones that started showing up last time in that area."

"Did you tell Sheriff Lloyd?"

"Nope. She wouldn't look into the matter. What I found isn't enough to warrant her attention, especially with a murder to solve."

"But this paints a clear picture that Amelia is back. We have to tell her!"

"Look, Reynolds, I'll worry about the sheriff. With what we have right now, it's nothing more than trespassing. We need to more evidence that can tie it to Amelia Doss before Sheriff Lloyd will entertain it."

"But she knows Amelia is real—she was there last time. Surely, she'd understand now."

"She's the sheriff now. Has to play politics, can't just do things on a whim like before."

"God dammit, but we know what's going on. We have to take this matter into our hands."

"I'd slow your roll. It's still possible it was just an animal desperate for a hiding spot in that mine."

Tyler threw his head back and laughed, seeming to mock James. "An animal? Okay, right. I'm sure it's just Smokey the Bear lounging around. C'mon."

"Look, Reynolds, I believe it was Amelia Doss, too—don't mistake my hesitancy for thinking otherwise. But we need more than this. Sure, we can assume she is responsible for the murder, but so what? How do we actually capture her? How can we ensure everyone in your life is safe, and we won't have an incident like last time? She has abilities, she moves in the night. Just because we know it's her doesn't mean this is going to be simple. We need a plan, and careful steps to follow to keep everyone safe. Do you understand?"

"Yes." Tyler couldn't stand still, constantly looking over his shoulder as if he expected his wife to open the door and call him out for agreeing to such a dangerous adventure. "Danny has been looking into the matter. We're meeting for dinner tomorrow night to discuss what he's found. Would you want to come?"

"How long have you two been talking about this?" James asked, peering into Tyler, displeased that they had already started taking matters into their own hands.

"Just recently," Tyler said, looking to the ground like a shamed child. "At least in serious terms. We talk about her all the time—it's only natural."

"I really hope you haven't planned anything. It's too dangerous."

"We haven't. Danny has done some more research and thinks that it is time to make a plan—that's what we're meeting about to discuss."

"I have to discourage that from happening."

This caused Tyler's head to shoot up, eyes blazing with anger. "Well, it's happening. And you're still invited. We could definitely use your help."

James sighed, suddenly itching for a cigarette. He patted his pockets, knowing he had none, but did so out of habit. His mouth grew dry. "Okay. I'll join you. I suppose someone needs to be there to talk some sense into you boys when you plan to go in over your head."

"We're not kids anymore. Any plan will be carefully thought out. We can't afford to be reckless again."

"Well, that's at least a good sign. I'm gonna get back home, and I hope you'll try to keep your mind at ease tonight. She can't stay on the run forever—we'll get her."

James offered these final words of encouragement before nodding his head and turning down the pathway to his truck parked on the curb. He wondered if they could actually catch Amelia Doss. Perhaps she could, indeed, stay on the run forever. She had lasted this long without so much as a close call, the town only spreading her legend, strengthening her, according to Tyler and Danny.

"Thanks for checking in, Mr. Abbott," Tyler called from the porch once James reached the sidewalk.

He looked over his shoulder with a soft grin. "Anytime, young man. You keep that family of yours safe, and I'll see you tomorrow. Let me know the details."

James sat down in his truck and fired up the engine, his stomach dancing cartwheels as a faint throb of adrenaline flowed through his arms and fingers. He had been retired and out of the game, but suddenly felt called back in for one last case. A case that meant so much for the town of Ridgeway and to him. He still had a chance to catch the one that got away.

❧ 15 ❧

Finding places to hide was a lot easier the more Amelia did it. Sometimes she hid under Tyler and Avery's bed. Other times just beyond the reach of the light in the same room. Had the living looked closer, they would have noticed the human-shaped shadow figure standing behind them while they sat on the couch or glimpsed her in a dark corner of the room watching them. Following Tyler to work proved more difficult. There, she had to shove her wisp of a form beneath the seats and settle into the darkness there. She was convinced that once she hit the light, she'd manifest again.

On this day, she was alone. Azazoth had stayed behind to watch over the nest of shadows in the attic, to keep them from mischief, presumably, while she hitched a ride with Tyler to work. The drive, while tedious, didn't take too long, and Amelia waited until he left the car before she popped out of her hiding spot and looked around. It was still too early for students to arrive. She exited the car through the ventilation system, then drifted along the cold pavement and concrete walkways toward the school, appearing like a floating mist to anyone passing by. The other teachers paid her no attention. Not even when she slipped in behind them and made her way along the corridors of the High School, checked out dark classrooms and closets, and reacquainted herself with the layout of the building. They had built it up a bit since the last time she was here. With Ridgeway growing, it made sense that the school would have to expand, too.

Finally, she found herself in the administration office, and slid between two filing cabinets to listen.

The ringing telephone and nasally voice of the recep-tionist grew weary after a short time, so she dove to the ground and slid along it like a snake, and then went under a door into an office that felt more comfortable. Behind the desk sat a balding man with a mustache and glasses, his eyes focused intently on the papers in his hands. Amelia slid into the far, shadowed corner, and stood behind the coat-rack, watching. The man shook his head and let out a heavy sigh. Then his phone rang.

"Yes? Ah, I see. Well, schedule a meeting with him." Pause. "Oh, all right. Send him in."

The door opened, and Amelia's eyes widened. It was Tyler.

"Mr. Reynolds! Tyler. Good morning."

"Principal Ambrose." Tyler took the chair on the opposite side of the desk without being asked.

"Call me Bill. We'll save the formality for the kids. How are your classes going so far?"

"Great. It seems I have a good group of kids this year." He nodded.

"I heard you had an issue with the media station in your classroom," Mr. Ambrose said.

"Yeah, Joe got it fixed. Loose wire apparently." Tyler looked around the office and shook his head. "It's so strange how things have changed. I remember this office not being nearly as comfortable or homey when I was a student here.”

Mr. Ambrose laughed. “Well, my predecessor kept it stark. There’s also the perspective…”

Tyler nodded. “So, you wanted to see me?”

“I just wanted to check in with you about Sam Murphy. He’s not really a problem student, but his parents are worried he’s been moody lately. Does he seem to be doing okay in class?” There was a look of concern plastered on the principal’s face.

“That’s most teenagers, isn’t it?” Tyler paused, as if waiting for a reaction. When none came, he continued. “He seems bright, inquisitive, and pretty normal, but I’ll keep an eye on him.”

“Good. Sam’s father is a friend of mine. We play golf sometimes. I keep eyes on his kids. Better to nip a problem in the ass before it gets out of hand, if you follow.” Mr. Ambrose stood.

“Yes. Absolutely. I suppose when mine get to be that age, I’d hope someone would watch out for them, too.” Tyler stood, too.

“How has the move gone?”

“We’re getting settled. Most everything is unpacked.”

“I heard your neighbor was killed.” It wasn’t a question. Bill Ambrose appeared to be seeking details.

“We never really knew him, but yeah. Sad.”

Then Ambrose twisted his mouth. “Murder seems to follow you.”

Amelia was sure she saw Tyler gulp, and she stifled a snicker.

“Coincidence, I’m sure,” Tyler said, not sounding entirely convinced.

“Well, let’s hope so. Glad to hear you’re settling in. I

expect to see you at the staff meeting on teacher planning day," he said.

"Of course. It's going to be the highlight of the week," Tyler said with just a touch of sarcasm.

Bill Ambrose laughed. "Yours and mine both." Then he stretched out his hand to Tyler. They shook hands, and Tyler left the office.

Amelia stayed in the office, listening. When she finally tired of Bill Ambrose, she slipped out and continued her exploration of the high school. Twice she was taken for a mist rising on the floor, and a couple of students and teachers did a double take when they saw her incorporeal form floating across an open walkway, but not once did anyone suspect Amelia Doss.

She spent some time in the Algebra class next door to Tyler's classroom before finally slipping into Tyler's room and lodging herself behind two filing cabinets in the back. The one-inch space was not a problem when she was in mist form, able to slip into the tiniest of holes and crevices. While watching Tyler rarely bored her, watching him teach did. So, she checked out the dark places in maintenance. Exploration of the building kept her so busy that she'd completely lost track of the hours, and by the time she emerged back into the main corridors, the sun was setting and the school was practically empty. Amelia made her way back to the now empty administration office. Something about Bill Ambrose beckoned her. He was still sitting at his desk when she crept under the door. Tyler was right. Ambrose's office was more comfortable and homier, but it was missing something.

A sly smile crept onto Amelia's transparent lips. The sun was going down, and Bill had turned off the overhead light and was working by a small desk lamp. This gave Amelia ample room to move around, just outside the reaches of the light. He took off his glasses and rubbed his eyes. Then he stood, stretched, and looked over to the coat-rack. "Another day down," he said to no one.

As he strode across the room to grab his coat, Amelia turned herself solid, this time replete with razor-sharp claws. Before he saw her, she grabbed his right leg and yanked it from underneath him, sending him sprawling to the floor with a thud. His glasses flew from his face, landing two feet in front of him near the coat-rack.

"Son of a bitch," he mumbled, trying to get his arms and legs beneath him so he could get up.

Amelia, now in full physical form, jumped on his back, shoving her dagger-like claws through his clothing and into his flesh, reaching inside to find his beating heart.

He let out a single cry before Amelia reached through his ribcage and grabbed his heart, squeezing it with such ferocity that it turned to pulp in his chest. Bill Ambrose stopped moving immediately and Amelia slid her hand from his chest cavity, then rolled him over.

The man's eyes were wide with shock, his lips parted as if he'd wanted to scream but it was so sudden, he couldn't. Amelia cleared the desk, shoving everything to the floor with the sweep of her arm.

With little effort, she lifted the two-hundred-and-fifty-pound man and placed him on his back, on the desk, and ripped open his dress shirt. Buttons flew everywhere.

"It's time to redecorate," Amelia said, a maniacal grin on her lips. With his chest and stomach bared before her, she turned her right index finger into a knife. It was so strange how she could do such a thing, but it made it so she didn't have to carry weapons with her. While she missed her axe, and her knife from all those years ago, she didn't miss having to lug either around.

With her knife-finger she sliced into Bill Ambrose's stomach, careful to drag through the fat and muscle until she reached the body cavity. Then, gingerly, she scooped out the intestines and set them next to the principal's body. Half of them toppled over and slopped to the floor with a wet slurp. She left them and began pulling out the organs she could reach: the liver, the stomach, the kidneys, and the bladder. She left the lungs and his destroyed heart muscle. Once she'd excised them all from the body cavity, she placed each kidney on either side of the shelf, as if they were matching bookends. She set the liver on the windowsill. The bladder, still full of urine, she placed on top of one filing cabinet and put the stomach on the other.

Amelia then turned her attention to the intestines. She took the end she'd removed from the stomach in one hand, a stapler in the other, and started at one end of the room. Elongating herself so she didn't need a chair or a ladder, she stapled the free end of the intestine high on the wall, near the ceiling. She let a bit drape, as if it were a garland, and stapled another section near the ceiling. She went all around the room like this, and then began stapling Bill Ambrose's intestines to the ceiling, leaving some dangling to give the effect of hanging crepe paper. She ran out of staples with only half the ceiling done. It was no matter—the finished effect was astounding. Blood and feces slid down the walls and dripped from the ceiling.

She smiled at her handiwork. "This is much better," she whispered. Looking down at her blood and shit-stained hands, she willed them clean and cackled to herself before shifting into her ethereal form and leaving the office, and the high school, behind her. The entire way back to the attic, she giggled to herself, imagining the looks on people's faces when they saw Principal Ambrose so meticulously dissected and his office decorated. She couldn't wait to get back to the attic to Azazoth and the others, to tell them what she had done. They would appreciate her hard work.

Halfway home, she realized she hadn't eaten. Not one drop of Bill Ambrose's blood went into her mouth, and yet she didn't feel hungry. In fact, she felt quite satisfied. It was as if the fear the man exuded when she clenched his raw heart had seeped into her very being, replenishing her strength and vitality. She slipped out of the shadows and began skipping down the street, happy and carefree in that moment of pure bliss. When she reached the Reynolds house, her heart sank a bit. It was back to reality and the real reason she was here. She eased up the side of the house and into the vent, finding the den of shadows quite cozy and inviting.

They must have smelled the blood on her because they all turned toward her as she arrived.

Azazoth, his big grin with jagged teeth, approached her. "What have you done, Amelia?" But it wasn't accusatory. There was a mischievous tone to the question.

"I helped Tyler's boss decorate his office," Amelia said, unable to hide her own grin.

The shadows all began to cackle, as if death was such an amusing thing. For *them*, it was.

16

Tyler paced, his stomach twisting into several knots. He had mentioned in the morning, before heading out for work that he would go to dinner with Danny tonight.

"Why can't he come here to eat?" Avery had asked while they both dressed for the day.

"We need to discuss something in private. It's about our past."

"About Amelia?" Avery had asked, crossing her arms and studying her husband.

"No," Tyler lied, refusing to let his wife open that door. "It's something I'll have to explain later."

Avery had grunted and shook her head before storming out of the bedroom. "You can drop the kids off today," she had said, leaving the house without another word and slamming the door shut to prove a point.

Now, at the tail end of the day, Tyler returned home from work to find his wife cooking dinner while the kids colored at the kitchen table behind her. She hadn't messaged him all day like she normally did. He called her on his lunch break, only for her to not answer.

He dropped his briefcase next to the coat-rack and braced for another round of shouting. The worst part was that he understood perfectly well why she was upset, even agreed with it. But the last thing he needed was his entire family to be worried about a serial killer who they had yet to prove was back in Ridgeway, no matter how overwhelmingly he believed it as truth.

He inched toward the kitchen's entryway, keeping his steps silent, until strolling in with a fake confidence.

"Hey, kids!" Tyler greeted, hanging his smile wide with delight as his children hopped out of their seats to smother him with hugs around his thighs. It also helped soften the blow surely coming his way from Avery. "How was everyone's day?" he asked, also faking the chipper undertones in his voice.

"Good, Daddy!" Charlotte cried out, quickly returning to her throne at the table, a coloring book of Cinderella with blue scribbles across the page splayed open. Wyatt returned to his place without a word.

"How was your day?" Tyler asked in Avery's direction, her back still facing him as she cooked over the stovetop.

"Fine," she replied. "Just cooking dinner for three."

She spoke with no emotion, a key indicator that she was still in a sour mood. Tyler didn't know how to respond, and looked to his feet as he tried to figure it out.

"What are you making?" he asked.

She didn't answer, but he could clearly see the empty package of spaghetti noodles lying on the counter, the jar of marinara right next to it.

"What time is dinner with your *friends?*" Avery asked, sure to fling her condescending tone across the room.

"I have to leave in an hour."

"How kind of you to spend some time with us before you leave."

"Avery, please. I swear I'll tell you what's going on as soon as I can."

"Okay. Have fun."

Avery's rage had grown palpable in the kitchen, to the point Tyler decided to not approach any closer as long as the pot of boiling water was the nearest thing she could grab.

"Avery, please. Can we talk?"

"Well, geez, Ty, can we? Does that work with your busy schedule? Sure you don't need to run off to dinner? Or go make another private phone call in the office? Make sure to close the doors so no one can hear you!"

Tyler shook his head, anger brimming within himself now that his wife had attacked him in such an accusatory tone. He knew meeting her fire of his own would only result in a messy shouting match in front of the kids. She clearly had strong emotions toward his recent activity, so he backed down for the peace of the household.

"Okay," he said. "Let's step into the other room and have a discussion."

Avery rolled her eyes before placing a lid over the boiling noodles and setting a timer for ten minutes, crossing her arms as she led the way out of the kitchen and into the living room. She planted her foot and pivoted around, facing Tyler with her lips pursed so tight together they had turned white.

"Babe, I'm sorry about tonight. I just hope you'll understand."

"Understand what? That men have needs? Sorry I don't want to climb on top of you every night—I'm fucking exhausted from working and keeping the house in shape and caring for the kids."

"Whoa! Where is this coming from?" Tyler felt the heat

radiating from his wife. He kept an arm's length distance between the two of them. "This isn't about the dinner, is it?"

"You tell me. Do you actually have dinner with your mistresses before you fuck them? Or do you just go over and get it started?"

"What?! You think I'm cheating on you?! Why the hell would you think that?"

"Really, Ty? Secret phone calls, late nights in your office on the computer, probably more phone calls. Staying late after work. I have no idea what you're really doing. All I can assume is that you found someone to satisfy you since I don't have the energy."

Avery's face flushed red, tears streaming down her cheeks.

"Oh my God," Tyler said, softening his tone as he stepped toward his wife and threw his arms around her. "This is not it at all, Avery. I think you've completely misread the situation. Not even close. I love you—I don't have eyes for anyone else in the world. Are you kidding me?"

He squeezed, her body trembling within his embrace as she fought off more tears.

"Then what is it?" she asked. "Because you're being very secretive."

While the bout of crying surely wasn't a strategic move, Avery had backed Tyler into a corner. He couldn't, in good faith, continue to hide the truth of what he had been up to over the last couple of weeks. He needed to spill the reality and only hoped she could handle it. He looked over his shoulder to make sure the kids hadn't shifted to the doorway to eavesdrop.

"It's her," Tyler whispered.

"Her who? Amelia Doss?" Avery asked, her tears clearing up, eyes still red and puffy as the last remnants of liquid pooled on the tip of her nose.

Tyler nodded. "I hope you can understand why I didn't

tell you. I didn't want you to be scared, especially in front of the kids. And because we're not even one hundred percent sure yet."

"Jesus, Ty, you should have just told me. Why would you leave me in the dark on something like this? Shouldn't I be prepared to defend myself and the kids?"

Tyler had always debated this matter. Was it worth having his wife on a constant edge just so she might have to fight off Amelia Doss on her own? He always assumed he'd be around when Amelia showed her face, but that hadn't been the case fifteen years ago when she kidnapped his mother. Both he and Danny were convinced that Amelia was done playing games, but the recent activity—should they confirm it as Amelia's fault—suggested otherwise. A dead dog, the dead principal, and the dead neighbor were not a dead Tyler Reynolds. The games were back on.

"I'm sorry. That's my fault. I thought this was something I could handle myself, at least within our house. I've fought her off once before, and I can do it again. I just worry because you don't fully understand what you're dealing with. Amelia isn't quite human, even though she might trick you into believing so."

"Then what are we supposed to do?" Avery asked. "Should we go to your parents' house? Your mom knows what to do, right? Is Amelia only coming here because she knows where we live?"

"Slow down. That's what we're trying to figure out. We're still waiting to see what the police say about Chad's death. If they have an actual suspect, then we can eliminate it being Amelia, and that will make us all feel much better. If they can't find one, then we have to assume it was her. It all follows a similar pattern. She kills those around me, inching ever closer. The same thing happened in college when she killed my roommate, and of course in high school when she killed my teacher and my friend."

"Why hasn't she just gone for you? It seems like she could have, whenever?"

Tyler shrugged. "We think that belief in her strengthens her. Our theory is that, since we've bested her once before, she wants to be as strong as possible before facing us again. She knows we know about her, and are ready."

"Did she kill Buster, or do you still think an animal did that?"

Tyler nodded. "I'm pretty sure that was her."

Avery squealed and slapped her hands over her face. "She's been in our house, Ty? Are you serious?!"

Tyler waved his hands, gesturing for her to quiet down. "Like I said, we don't know for sure. I highly doubt she was in our house in a physical form. She can move through walls like a ghost, and can make things happen paranormally. She's somehow supernatural now, we think."

She shook her head viciously from side to side. "So what now, Ty? I'm supposed to have dinner with the kids, and pretend none of this is happening? While you leave us alone?"

"You'll be fine—I promise. Just don't answer the door for strangers. Don't even answer the phone if it's not someone you know. Stay together with the kids until bedtime, and I'll be back by then. Besides, I don't think she's ever made a move during the day—all of her attacks have come late in the night. Just try to keep a clear head, okay?"

Avery nodded, sniffling as she wiped away the remaining tears from her face. Her eyeliner left the slightest streak along her cheek, and Tyler wiped that away with a quick stroke of his thumb.

"I hope you can understand why I wanted to keep this a secret," Tyler said. "I was afraid this is how you might respond. I didn't want you to have to feel this way, especially while we don't have all the facts."

"I'm sorry I accused you," Avery replied. "That wasn't fair. But you said it wasn't about Amelia Doss, and I believed you. That left me to piece together my own story."

"I love you. I'd never do anything like that to you and the kids. In fact, I'm doing all this *for* you and the kids—to keep you all safe. We have a lot of life ahead of us, and I plan to keep it that way."

"Should we just move away, Ty? Go as far as we can get from Ridgeway?"

"I'm afraid it's not that simple. It's not Ridgeway she's drawn to—it's me. No matter where I go, she'll always find me. The advantage of being in Ridgeway is that we know roughly where she *should* be. Less likely for surprises that way."

"Okay, I'll just trust you."

"Thank you. Now, I have to get going. Since it's all out in the air now, I hope we don't have to discuss this any further. I'm not going to tell you all the happenings of my discussion with Sheriff Abbott and Danny—but it's for the best, I promise. I *will* tell you things you need to know, for your safety. Does that work for you?"

"Yes. You also need to tell me where you're going, if you're going somewhere. You don't have to say for what reason, but I just need to know where you are. For your safety."

"Fair enough. Consider it done."

The two hugged, Tyler planting a kiss on top of his wife's head before they pulled apart and returned to the kitchen. Avery returned to the stove where the timer she had set was about to chime. Tyler moved around the table and kissed his kids goodbye, promising to be back in time to tuck them into bed. He did the same for Avery.

"Be safe," she whispered under her breath.

17

Tyler's house wasn't built on a relocated cemetery or old burial grounds. It wasn't built on sacred Native American land. As far as Danny's research went, it appeared the land had been nothing more than unspoiled mountain property. This led Danny to believe it wasn't a haunting at all, and while true, all the incidents Tyler and Avery had experienced in the house could be explained, mostly, with logic. Earlier that day, the story broke across town that Bill Ambrose, Tyler's boss, had been murdered in his office at the school. That made two murders now, and no matter how unrelated they seemed, it screamed Amelia Doss. Because, as the sheriff had pointed out at their recent meeting, the common factor was Tyler. And the minute the current sheriff figured that out, Tyler and the old murders would be brought up again. Chad Gunther was Tyler's neighbor. Bill Ambrose was Tyler's boss. But Amelia's MO had changed, which led the current sheriff and deputies to believe they were looking for two separate murders. James Abbott hoped to keep it that way, at least until they'd gotten rid of Amelia.

James had finally told Tyler about the dead animals and the disturbance of the old mine. Now, the three of them planned to meet regularly until they figured out how to be rid of Amelia once and for all.

From Danny's point of view, Amelia appeared to be trying to throw law enforcement off by being unpredictable, or she was experimenting with something new. He thought of how Ambrose had been found and grabbed his stomach. It made him sick just thinking about it. Bad news in a small town traveled fast, and he knew they really had found the man with his intestines hung like Christmas garlands around his office.

Amelia had stopped being predictable fifteen years ago. She was stealthier now, but how? Danny lifted an eyebrow. Was it possible Amelia had finally shed any mortality and was now stuck in this world as a vengeful spirit? Perhaps the ritual he'd done fifteen years ago had only stripped her of a body. He knew one person who would know, and Tyler and the ex-sheriff had tasked him with figuring out the metaphysical side of the matter since he had friends who were *into that sort of thing*, as James Abbott put it.

That's why Danny cleared his schedule and picked up the phone to call Lavinia, his friend in Denver who ran *Dark Works*. Lavinia always answered Danny's call, provided he didn't call too late. They'd developed an interesting friendship over the years. Even when he just wanted someone to talk to, to bounce novel ideas off, Lavinia was always there. She seemed to enjoy talking about his books and life in Ridgeway. In a strange way, they could live vicariously through one another. Lavinia an urban witch, business owner, and coven leader—and Danny a small-town horror writer and museum volunteer.

She picked up on the third ring. "Hey, Danny." She sounded glad to hear from him.

"Have I rescued you from something, or interrupted you?" he asked.

Her laughter lifted his spirits. "Really, I was just doing laundry, so rescued?"

He laughed. "Hey, you remember back when we first met when I did that ritual to get rid of..."

Lavinia finished the sentence for him. "That devil?" That was the nature of city girls like Lavinia. They could steamroll a conversation.

"Yeah."

"Oh, shit." She got quiet for a moment and said, "She's back, isn't she?"

Whenever she did that, it sent a chill up Danny's spine. Lavinia somehow always knew why he was calling, and she would say things he hadn't told her. It was a matter of habit with her. "Yeah."

"When you told me your friend was moving back, I wondered if she'd show up again." She let out a heavy sigh. "Let me pour myself a glass of chardonnay and get comfortable for this conversation." He imagined her lithe form draped in Gothic fashion pouring herself a glass of deep red wine, her long black nails glinting in the light against the dark amber wine bottle. He listened to the clinking, the walking, and Lavinia settling into her favorite chair. Finally, she said, "Okay, I'm all ears. What's going on?"

"The first sign was he started having haunting and poltergeist activity in his house."

"Ooh. Such as?" This sort of thing fascinated Lavinia. It scared the shit out of Danny.

"His wife saw a figure in their pantry. They woke up and all their chairs, like dining and kitchen table chairs, were moved. The kids are seeing ghosts. Then..." He drew in a deep breath. "Tyler found their dog dead in the basement.

Their neighbor was decapitated. A little while after that, his boss ended up dead, all his organs removed." He put his hand to his mouth as if it would keep him from getting sick at the thought of that latter detail.

Lavinia was stone cold, silent for a minute. "Good gods." Then, he could tell that she took a long drink of the wine.

"I mean, do you still think it's a demon? Or devil, rather? Is it possible I only separated her from a physical body?" He grabbed the olive-green lap blanket from the back of his couch and threw it over his shoulders to fight the chill rising within him.

"Yeah. Definitely still a devil. But it sounds like she's changed, and it could be because of the ritual you did." There was a hint of apology for the last part.

"Changed? How?" The sound of his own terrified voice startled him.

"Well, if she started as a physical being—not all devils do— then being physical was probably the most comfortable form for her. But then she learned how to change into a wraith-like creature that can slip through the night like a mist or a shadow." Anytime Lavinia talked about the occult, her voice had this foreboding tone to it that made Danny shudder a little. Then he heard her swallow. "Danny? I'm really scared for you."

"Why?"

"Devils don't like it when people interfere. This one is there to take out your friend, and I'm worried it's going to take out anyone that stands in its way. Do you still have that necklace you got from the shop?" she asked.

He hadn't seen that obsidian necklace in years. Had he given it to Tyler? Had Tyler given it back? He honestly didn't remember. "I don't think so." Thinking he saw a dark shadow near the front door, his eyes darted over there. It was nothing. "So how do we fight something we can't see?"

"I think the first step would be to ward your house, and Tyler's, and any other place you want to keep her out of." Then she took another drink, and he heard her set down the wine glass. "Usually where there's one devil, there are more. So, she may not be working alone."

His eyes widened. "Wait, what?"

"Like attracts like, especially negativity." Then her voice got louder. "First, protection, then you can start figuring out how to get rid of her. Are we sure she's not actually attached somehow to Tyler?"

"I don't think so..."

"I mean, does he have anything of hers? Because for two rituals to only get rid of her temporarily tells me she's either attached to him, or to something else that was hers in life." Lavinia waited.

That's when the image of the axe rushed back in a flood of memories. "The axe. She used it to kill everyone all those years ago, back when we were in high school. I'm quite sure it's still in the police evidence lockup."

She perked up. "Can you get it?"

He furrowed his brow. "Not without help from the retired sheriff. I'm sure he still has friends in the department. Whether they'll give it to him is another matter, since it's still considered a cold case. It's not like they'll let us waltz in and take a pivotal piece of evidence that could someday catch their killer."

"Can the sheriff steal it?"

A laugh tumbled from him, unbidden. The mere thought of James Abbott tiptoeing through the Ridgeway Sheriff Department's evidence lockup in the dead of night was rather amusing. "I don't think he's the type. Real law-abiding and all that, and retired. However, he might be able to convince them to let us borrow it."

"Well, you're going to have to take it back to her grave and destroy it."

"Destroy *evidence?*" Danny could hear James having a fit, even now. That was the thing with long-time law enforcement. They had solid ideas of right and wrong, legal, and illegal, and they couldn't be convinced that under the right set of circumstances, doing one illegal thing might ultimately be in everyone's best interests.

"Obviously, you aren't going to tell him you're going to destroy it."

"Are you sure she's attached to something?"

Lavinia's voice became firm. "Yes. It's either a thing, like the axe, or it's Tyler."

"Shit. If it's Tyler, I'm not going to have to destroy him, am I?"

"No. Exorcism by a shaman who knows how to remove a spirit attachment could work." Lavinia left a thoughtful pause between them before saying, "Though I suppose you could do it. Let's try the axe first."

"Can't I try them both at once? Because seriously—I don't think we should drag this out. How many more people are going to die?" Danny clenched his hands into fists. "Like you said, anyone between Amelia and Tyler could be next. That could be Avery. Or one of the kids. Or James Abbott. Even me." Though deep down, he had a feeling he was low on Amelia's priority list. She was more likely to go after Avery first, just to get to Tyler. Then the kids... He shuddered again.

"I suppose that's not a bad idea. But will Tyler agree to it?"

"If anyone is willing to try anything to get rid of her, Tyler would be the one."

"Good. I'm going to email you some information." She sat quietly on the other end of the line for a few more moments. "Are you okay, Danny?"

He let out a heavy sigh. "I don't know. I have a lot going on. This new book has to be sent to my editor month after next. We're getting ready to shift out the main part of the Amelia Doss exhibit at the museum."

"Wait, you're getting rid of it?" She sounded impressed.

"Yeah, my co-worker convinced the museum board we can scale it down to a few items in the display case, and not an entire wall."

"That might help, especially if people's belief in her feeds her power." Lavinia's voice had a hint of hope in it.

"Good point, but will it be enough? I mean, it's not like Ridgeway's residents sit around ruminating over the Amelia Doss incident that happened a hundred years ago." He narrowed his eyes. "She also feeds on blood, though. Which is why I initially thought she was some kind of vampire."

"It's not as simple as that. Devils can feed on fear, belief, and blood. Probably a few other things, but those are the three off the top of my head." She probably shrugged after saying this, or at least in Danny's imagination she did.

"So, we take away the belief and all we have is fear and blood."

"Things that go bump in the night," Lavinia added.

"Hence the whole ghost thing. The murders and the ghosts. Fear and blood. It's like every time we take away something she can use to get stronger, she finds something else." He glanced at the clock, realizing it was already past ten. He was running the museum by himself the following day.

"It's a combination of things. I'll email you what you'll need tonight. *Don't* take your time—set up the ritual as soon as you can. It means getting the axe and bringing Tyler on board, but one of those things has to work." Then her voice softened. "Until then, get some rest. I'll send you information about warding your house. I'd send you more amulets, but gods only know if you'll get them in time."

Danny nodded. "Thanks, Lavinia. I don't know what I'd do without you."

"I'll talk to you later, Danny."

That night, he slept with the lights on.

18

Danny didn't notice that Amelia had been listening to his entire conversation with the witch. Well, his side, at least. The gist of it wasn't lost on her. They were trying to come up with a plan to send her back beyond the grave again. There was mention of her axe, and of Tyler, and that relentless sheriff. She'd been hiding behind the couch, so close to Danny she could have reached out and touched him with a ghostly hand. Back in her day, witchcraft was unheard of. Now, it was one more thing that made this new world vile and beyond salvation. Just as she knew he would, Danny Espinoza was inserting himself between her and Tyler—again. Amelia decided that if Danny wanted a fight, she'd give him one. But what made her the angriest was when she heard they were downsizing her role in Ridgeway. Years ago, after she'd first returned, she'd visited the Ridgeway Museum and seen the wall of memories they'd erected to her. It was more than she'd ever hoped for. But now they planned to take it down and relegate her to a few false items: an axe that wasn't even hers, and maybe a fuzzy photograph in a glass display case. The nerve.

She left his house before he went to bed and returned to the Reynolds' attic, sulking.

Azazoth, as usual, knew exactly what was happening. He could read her emotions and thoughts as if she printed them on a billboard. "Kill him."

That was Azazoth's answer to everything. While it sounded tempting, feeding off of Danny's fear until he was too weak to perform witchcraft sounded even better. She may not have been a vampire, but there was no reason she couldn't behave like one. In her mind, she visualized sucking his life force from him, leaving him a shell of a man with dark, sunken in eyes, staring at a white wall. Yes, that sounded like a fitting end to an annoying obstacle like Danny Espinoza. "I'll visit Danny tomorrow. Give him one hell of a fright." A sly grin slid over her lips. "There is no way he will ruin this for me."

Azazoth nodded slowly. "Yes, Amelia."

SHE WAITED UNTIL LATE AFTERNOON BEFORE LEAVING THE Reynolds residence. The museum wasn't that far away, and it only took her fifteen minutes, dodging from shadow to shadow through the old streets of Ridgeway before reaching her destination. In the open areas she drifted upward, the unknowing residents assuming she was merely smoke from someone's cigarette, or exhaust from a building. Regardless, her movements didn't attract any attention, and she slipped under the museum door without detection.

It was much nicer inside. The museum was cool and, with subdued lighting, offered more varied hiding places. Danny Espinoza sat behind a back counter wearing a pair of reading glasses, his nose in a book. As he took notes, he'd pause every few minutes to adjust his glasses. Finally, he sat back, took the spectacles off, and rubbed his eyes with a sigh. Glancing at his watch, he stood and ambled across the recently cleaned floors, making his way to the door. He flipped over the sign from Open to Closed and turned the lock in the door, then leaned over to unplug the lights in the windows.

Amelia puzzled at this, wondering if the lights did anything for the museum or its patrons. Clearly, they'd been installed to draw people into the museum, but it obviously wasn't working. Danny made his way back to the counter and sat back down. "Amelia," he said.

She almost answered. Almost. Moving toward Danny, she kept low to the floor, where it was darker and unlikely to be spotted. Even in her stealthy approach, she noticed the Amelia Doss display had lost its luster since her last visit. A mere shell of its former glory. She stayed on the ground, on the opposite side of the counter where Danny continued reading.

With a giggle, she imagined herself popping up on her side of the counter and saying, "Boo!"

At the counter, Danny looked up toward the door. He probably thought the giggle had come from outside, and Amelia decided she would have to be more careful. She slipped along the floor, over to her display, and studied at the barren wall. Where her name had once been prominently painted on the upper half of the wall was now bare and gray, and a faint whiff of the fresh paint permeated the air.

Danny let out another deep sigh and Amelia turned toward him, only to find the man staring wistfully toward the front door, as if he saw something no one else could. He took his glasses off again and stood, moving to the register near the door where tickets were sold, and a few shelves of souvenirs stood on display. Going into the register, he removed the money and placed it in a bag that he must have taken from below the counter. Then he closed the register and retreated to the rear counter.

Amelia was a sitting duck. She shoved her shadow-self into the crevice just beneath the counter and watched as his tennis-shoe clad feet walked mere inches from her and he disappeared behind a curtain that led to a back room. Swooping out from her hiding spot, she reared up and over the counter, pausing to look at the book Danny was reading. It was a book titled *Exorcism: The Rites and Traditions of Spirit Removal*. A half-smile slid onto her lips and with a single thought, her hand and arm went from transparent to solid and she lifted the book and stood it up, then took Danny's glasses and balanced them with great care on top of it. She stood back and admired her handiwork, then looked around the large space filled with the artifacts of Ridgeway's history. What else could she move?

Her eyes spied a black marker behind the counter, and a grim plan surfaced. Taking up the marker, she uncapped it and moved to the now solid, empty wall. Did she write her name? No, she quickly decided. It was best to keep Danny guessing. Did she write some cryptic message like, *I'm back.* Or, *Hello, Danny.* While these options amused her, none felt right.

There was a shuffle in the back. Whatever she was going to do, she'd have to do it quickly. In a large, scrawling cursive, she wrote: *Ridgeway*. Danny's footfalls broke the silence and Amelia vanished, dropping the marker, which clattered to the floor. She retreated behind a pair of mannequins dressed in garments from the early 1900s.

Danny hurried from the back and looked around, his eyes first falling on the book and his glasses on the counter. His audible gasp filled the room. "What the hell?" His eyes settled on the marker on the floor and followed up to the word *Ridgeway* written on the wall. "Son of a bitch. Who's here?" His eyes darted around the museum, searching every display, every possible hiding place. "You've gotta be kidding me," he said under his breath. He went to the front of the museum and checked the locked door, then disappeared into the back again, only to emerge even more baffled than before.

"Who's here?" he called again into the empty museum.

Amelia just watched, not moving an inch from her space behind the mannequins.

Danny returned to the book and his glasses, then glared at the writing on the wall. "Dammit."

Amelia had half a mind to tell him to watch his mouth in front of a lady, but again kept this to herself. In the modern world, it seemed people cursed as reflexes to their situation, and Danny was no exception. She watched with mild amusement as he retrieved a can of gray paint and a paint roller to paint over the word Ridgeway. He finished and went to the back, and Amelia took the time to move some displays around, undress one mannequin, leaving its clothes a heap on the floor, and completely rearranging the souvenirs.

Upon his return, he immediately noticed the undressed mannequin. But this time, she could feel his trepidation. It tasted so sweet.

While he re-dressed the mannequin and his back was to her, she whispered, "Danny."

He whirled around, hands up like he was ready for a fight.

She giggled.

"Amelia?"

How did he know? Amelia wondered if she should respond. Even if he instinctively knew it was her, if she gave him confirmation, it meant she'd have him on her heels from hereon out. She narrowed her eyes and her attention moved to the museum display of a woman named Leslie Wilcox, an early owner of the Ridgeway Saloon. "Leslie," she whispered. Her voice sounded so distant and soft, not like her mortal voice at all. Whether or not Danny would believe a spirit named Leslie was haunting the museum was another story.

Danny's brow furrowed, as if he hadn't been able to make out what she'd said, but this expression soon vanished when his eyes fell on the muddled souvenir display. He moved over to the souvenir shelves and began sorting the cups, hats, and key chains. When he finished, he turned back toward the center of the museum. "Please stop making more work for me. Instead, why not tell me why you're here?" Uncertainty flashed in his eyes.

"Leslie Wilcox," she whispered.

Danny's eyes lowered to the display that mentioned Leslie Wilcox. He just stood there, not saying anything. "I know it's you, Amelia. What do you want?"

The jig was up. Until Tyler was finally dead, she was going to have Danny Espinoza on her tail. If she wanted to finish what she'd come back for, she'd have to stay a few steps ahead of him.

"Come on. Don't be shy. What do you want?"

"I'm watching you," she spat at him.

"And I you," he returned.

The petulant nerve of the man! When she'd first met Danny, he'd been a scrawny kid who'd practically pissed himself the first time he saw her. She wondered if he was that same kid now, only older and more filled out. From the corner of her eye, she saw a pitchfork to her left. She reached out, grabbed it, and manifested. With her manifestation, the slightest odor of sulfur filled the room. "Catch this, Danny!" she said, and threw the pitchfork at him.

He turned toward her voice. His eyes went wide, and he veered to the side, the pitchfork merely grazing his upper bicep. His opposite hand immediately went to the wounded flesh. "Holy shit!"

Amelia stalked toward him, her gaze holding his. "Stay out of my way, or you're next."

Danny stumbled backward, tripping over the pitchfork and falling onto his backside with a hard thump.

She kept moving toward him, and he scooted away. "I'll enjoy killing you," she told him.

The sound of keys and a cool blast of air from the door pulled Amelia's attention away from Danny toward the door and the slack-jawed old woman who stood there.

Amelia vanished in a flash, her shadow slipping away into a dark corner.

"Danny, are you all right?" the woman rushed to him and helped him up.

While shaken, Danny regained his composure rather quickly. "Yeah, I'm fine. Thanks, Maryanne."

"What was that? Was that a ghost?" The woman's aging face displayed shock more than fear.

Danny swallowed, looking around to see if Amelia was still there. When he didn't see her, he turned back to the old woman. "You saw her, too?"

"Yes. It looked like a woman..." Then she stopped and sniffed the air. "It smells like something is burning."

"No, that's sulfur. The smell a demon—" He stopped himself mid-sentence.

The woman's eyes went wider. "I was passing, and I saw the light on and thought I'd stop in." Then her gaze settled on the pitchfork.

Danny immediately picked it up and put it back from where Amelia had retrieved it.

"I knew it," Maryanne said quietly. "I knew this place was haunted. Come on. Let's lock up and get out of here before anything else happens. We'll go to the diner and I'll buy you a cup of coffee."

"Yeah. Okay."

Together, Danny left with the old woman, leaving Amelia alone in the darkness. That hadn't gone as planned, and Amelia wondered just how much of a problem Danny was going to be this time around.

＊ 19 ＊

It was Friday night when Danny had called for an emergency meeting with Tyler and James. Yes, it was about Amelia, but he provided no other details. Tyler explained this to Avery, believing Danny had some sort of breakthrough. His friend had never before called for a meeting with such urgency.

Tyler hopped in his car and drove over to Danny's house. Danny had stated his desire to meet at his own home, wanting the freedom to roam his property and not worry about a nosy server overhearing their conversation. He arrived at Danny's place to find both him and James sitting on the front porch bench, each puffing a cigarette.

Tyler parked in the roundabout at the bottom of the porch steps and climbed up to meet them. "Dan? Everything okay? I don't think I've ever seen you smoke."

"Let's begin," Danny said, dismissing the question. He stood with the motion of a fragile old man, and Tyler noticed a slight tremble in his friend's hand, thanks to the cigarette bouncing in subtle movements.

Blood rushed into Tyler's chest and stomach as he sensed troubling news.

Danny popped the cigarette back into his mouth and took a long drag, blowing it to the trees above that served as a canopy over his isolated home. "I saw her last night," he finally said, promptly taking another drag.

"Amelia was here?!" Tyler asked.

Danny shook his head. "At the museum. I closed up last night, and once I was alone, she came in. Spiritually."

"How do you know?"

"Well, to start, I sensed someone in there with me. You know how you can feel when someone is staring at you? I had that the entire time once I was alone. I looked all over the place, but couldn't find anyone. Figured my mind was playing tricks on me. But then things started moving. A book, a marker. One of the mannequins was undressed."

"Jesus, Danny, she could have killed you!" Tyler gasped. "Alone in that building—you'd have no chance."

"I don't think she's strong enough," Danny said, blowing more smoke as his gaze fell to the sunset in the distance.

"You can't possibly know that," Tyler replied. "And one day, it'll be too late if you stick to that logic."

"I know," Danny said absentmindedly. "We spoke."

"What?!" Tyler snapped. "Why are you being so calm about this?"

Danny shrugged. "I don't feel calm. I feel like I'm on the verge of a panic attack. We need to kill her. Immediately."

"Did you know about this?" Tyler spun around and asked James, who had remained just as calm, tending to his cigarette and enjoying the sunset. If he hadn't known any better, Tyler would have thought the two of them were old friends catching up, talking about the good ol' days.

"Nope," James replied. "But I can't say I'm surprised.

We've met a couple times now, and it seems this should have been expected. Or am I mistaken?"

"Yes, of course, but why are we barely hearing about it now?" Tyler asked, pivoting back around to Danny. "Almost twenty-four hours after the fact. What the hell have you been doing all day?!"

"This," Danny said, sticking out his cigarette before taking another puff.

"The woman we are trying to hunt down *speaks* to you last night, and you thought it was best to spend the following day smoking a carton of cigarettes? Dan, I feel for you, but what the fuck?"

"Don't come at me like that," Danny snapped. "I've been the one carrying us. I do the dirty work, the hard research. For fuck's sake, I meet with witches to get answers. Would *you* ever walk up to a witch and start asking questions?"

"That's not the point! All of our lives are on the line. You saw or heard Amelia and didn't tell us until almost twenty-four hours after the fact? That's irresponsible. We need to all be on the same page and know what's going on."

"Ahhh, yes, the same page," Danny said, flicking his cigarette butt across the porch as his face lit up with a crazed grin. "Like in college, when you were almost killed by Amelia Doss, all so you could get laid? We were really on the same page, weren't we? Fortunately, I once again was so deep in research that I figured it all out just in time. Remind me, Ty, who saved you that day? Who kept you from getting carved up like a fucking jack-o'-lantern?!"

"Really, Dan? You want to bring up something that happened a lifetime ago? Fuck off!"

Tyler felt his face flushed with blood, his fists clenched into balls, fingernails digging into his sweaty palms.

James stood up and stomped his cigarette under his boot. "That's enough, boys. This is counterproductive. Danny didn't tell us last night, and there's nothing we can do about that now, so I suggest we drop the matter. Whatever happened in college is between you and also has nothing to do with the moment. There is a loose serial killer out there, and we need to find the best way to bring her down. If you have anything else to say outside of that matter, let me save you some time and tell you right now—I do not give a shit!"

James' tone had started off soft and gradually increased in intensity, nearly shouting by the end, making Tyler and Danny recoil and take a step back from the retired sheriff.

"I'm sorry I didn't tell either of you last night," Danny said, in a slightly quieter tone. "I just didn't know what to do, or what to think. Once I realized what was happening, it was like my life flashed before me. I had never really considered death before, and the thought of dying alone in the Ridgeway Museum sent my mind out of control. Today, I processed a lot more than Amelia, trust me. I've always thought I was just fine being alone in life, but that encounter last night has given me second thoughts. I'm just a crazy horror writer now, and maybe that's all I'll ever be remembered for. Kind of a sad life, once I had time to reflect on it."

James returned to his spot on the bench, pulling out another cigarette to light.

Tyler saw his friend in pain and stepped in to console him. "Dan, where is all this coming from? None of what you said is true. You may not have a wife or kids, but you're not alone in this world. Don't reduce your existence to your accomplishments. You've been a great friend my entire life, and if you really want a partner in life, then you'll find one. You've been so focused on your career—it's okay to take a step back and just live."

Danny, one to rarely show emotion, tilted his head downward in a move only Tyler knew was his version of crying. His eyes welled with tears, but he wiped them away before looking up. "Thanks, Ty. I've been so stressed with deadlines and this hectic schedule, and now Amelia. I just want her gone already."

"And that's what we're going to do."

James cleared his throat and stood back up. "Whenever you kids are done having your moment, I came over here to discuss catching a killer."

This earned a chuckle from Tyler and Danny, and Tyler slapped his friend on the back in a gesture of good faith.

"Okay," Danny said. "Let's talk."

"Before we do," James cut in. "Have you really been talking to witches, son? Like *real* witches?"

Danny laughed. "I have been. They're nothing like what I'm sure you believe them to be. No pointy hats, broomsticks, or crooked noses. They're just regular people who are really in tune with the spiritual side of the world."

James nodded quietly to himself, satisfied with the explanation.

"Well, what did they have to say?" Tyler asked.

"I've explained everything that's been going on, and everything we've tried so far. My friend Lavinia thinks Amelia has attached her soul to a physical object. This likely would have been done all those years ago when she first resurrected, so it's impossible to know what exactly. I like to think it's her axe—it only makes sense it would be something she keeps close by at all times."

"So we have to find her axe and destroy it?" James asked, puzzlement smothered across his face as Danny's explanation of souls being attached to items surely went right over his head.

"Correct. By having her soul attached to an object, it serves as a sort of protection for her. As long as the object is intact, we'll never truly be able to get rid of her, or send her back to the grave."

"But we don't know for sure what the object could be?" Tyler asked.

"Right. I'm making an assumption, but we can make a better guess by visiting the mine where she's been hiding and see if there is anything else it could be."

"Hold on a minute," James said. "You said this would have been done when she first came back?"

"Right, very likely."

"Well, we know she was living in Old Lady Myers' house for a good amount of time. We have a lot of things kept in storage from that crime scene, since it's still considered a cold case. I can try to get us in to that evidence room to have a look around."

"Brilliant!" Tyler said.

"In fact, I'm fairly certain the axe she used back then is with all that stuff."

Danny fell silent, nodding to himself as if he had just come to a grand revelation. "I think we can do this. In fact, it makes sense that it would be something in that evidence room. We chased her out of that basement—she didn't have time to grab things on her way out. The only she way might still have the object in her possession is if it was attached to her. Like a necklace or ring. Ty, you were up close and personal to her in your dorm room. Did she have any notable jewelry that you remember?"

Tyler thought back to that event where he had been stripped naked, while Amelia remained fully clothed as she tantalized his virgin desires. She had run her fingers all over his body, but she had no rings.

"Nothing that I recall. She always dressed pretty bland, never had anything flashy like jewelry."

Danny clapped his hands together in front of his face, his eyes drawn into the distance where the sun disappeared, casting an orange and purple mixture across the sky. "This actually brings everything into focus. The object, whatever it is, is very much a lifeline for Amelia. It's likely she attached it to something in that basement, and has been looking for it ever since. That explains why she hasn't killed Tyler, even though she's had the opportunity. Maybe she's looking for it, and must figure Tyler, and myself, can lead her to it. Mr. Abbott, how hard is it to get in and out of that evidence room without permission?"

"Impossible," James said. "There are two doors to pass through, and multiple cameras inside, running constantly. An alert system notifies if there is movement within the room outside of authorized visits."

"So even if Amelia knows where it is, she had no way of physically getting it out, there would be a response the second she moved the box, even if she did it as a ghost—or whatever the hell she is."

"How are we supposed to know what the object is, though?" James asked. "We can't just take everything, but can probably slip a couple of things out to destroy."

Danny pursed his lips and shrugged. "Trial and error, I suppose. I've learned a new chant that should definitely work in sending her back to the grave. We can destroy an object, try the chant, and see if it works—it should be an instant result, so we don't have to wait around for results."

"Let's try it, boys," James said. "I can only take one of you with me. Tomorrow. For now, I need to go home and get some rest. And for God's sake, if anyone encounters anything until then, please update the group."

James marched down the porch steps without another word, nodding to Tyler and Danny before he slipped behind the wheel of his truck and took off.

20

James arrived at the police station at eight o'clock the next morning, having spent the night unable to fall asleep. Witches, chants, ghosts. He couldn't wrap his mind around it all, despite having seen the century-old serial killer live in the flesh over a decade ago. She had single-handedly softened his closed-mindedness ever since that evening in the Myers basement, but the extracurriculars Tyler and Danny had discussed crossed every line of his beliefs.

James stayed in his parked truck when he arrived, opting to wait for Danny before stepping out. Once one police officer saw him, it would be a round of catching up and reminiscing, something he definitely had no time for. Instead, he leaned back and cranked up the radio, an eighties station playing the soothing voice of Belinda Carlisle.

He made it through an entire song before Danny pulled into the parking lot and came knocking on James' driver-side door. Dark bags decorated the young man's bloodshot eyes. If James hadn't known differently, he'd have assumed Danny had a bowl of drugs for breakfast instead of cereal.

James opened his door and hopped out of the truck, his knees cracking and groaning in protest. "Long night, Danny?"

Danny nodded. "Do I look that bad?"

"Not as bad as you might think. I just know what I'm looking at. Couldn't get much sleep myself. But don't worry, you're the crazy horror writer—it sort of fits your image."

Danny chuckled, but there was a clear absence of energy behind the laughter. "You sure this is okay? I don't want you to get in any trouble."

James laughed. "Trouble? I have an exhibit in the museum, son. I'm pretty sure if they had the funds, they'd put up a statue of me right in this parking lot. It would take a lot for me to get in trouble, especially when the sheriff used to be my deputy."

"Does she know you're here?"

"No, Rachel doesn't need to worry herself with these sorts of matters, especially on a Saturday morning. I'm sure she'll hear about it and come knocking on my door later this weekend. But even then, that will be just to pick my brain about everything going on. Let's head in."

James led the way, moving past Danny and crossing the parking lot, just as he had countless times in his life.

Forty years, he thought as he approached the glass double doors that entered the police station. *Four decades. Two score, as Lincoln would say.*

The nostalgia rushed James, dizzying to where he thought he might actually fall over and cause a scene. He had to slow down his feet, but more importantly his mind. Retirement brought plenty of time for reflection, and he had thought about this place so many times since turning in his badge. The early mornings and late nights. Weekends. His entire life dedicated to keep the town of Ridgeway safe. He often wondered if he had made a mistake by marrying his job instead of another human. He supposed, in his late age, that it was natural to wonder if the grass truly was greener on the other side. Life had its fill of forks in the road, and by the end, one could only look back and imagine where the other roads might have led. James didn't have regret for how his life turned out, but he still had plenty of curiosity.

"You okay, Mr. Abbott?" Danny asked, the two having stopped walking five steps shy of the entrance.

"Yes, sorry. Just been a while. Never thought I'd actually be back here on official business."

Danny offered a soft grin and patted James on the back, telling him to take his time.

James needed no more encouragement and marched forward, swinging the doors open like he had when he was the sheriff. They entered to a quiet lobby, a lone officer sitting behind the front desk with a pair of glasses perched on the tip of his nose as he read the news on his computer screen. He looked up and immediately jumped to his feet.

"Sheriff Abbott!" he gasped. "What are you doing here? Is everything okay?"

James raised a steady hand. "Relax, Simms. I was hoping you might buzz me back to the evidence room. This is my friend, Danny, and he's come across some information that might be helpful in a cold case from many years back. It may be a long shot, but I wanted to look into a couple of boxes."

"Of course," Simms said, tossing his reading glasses on the desk and patting his pockets for his keys. "Follow me."

The heavyset officer turned and started for the door behind his desk, James leading the way for Danny to follow. He led them down a hallway that had several doors on each side, mostly offices.

"It's been too long," Simms said when they reached the last door at the end. "How have things been?"

"I can't complain," James said. "Lots of golf and sitting around. The usual, I suppose."

"Is this cold case going to bring you out of retirement?" Simms asked with a childlike giddiness.

"Afraid not. Not something I'd be interested in taking back up, but if I find anything useful, I'll let Sheriff Lloyd know and see if she wants to pursue it."

"Abbott and Lloyd back together," Simms said, dismissing the ex-sheriff's last comment. "You two are legends."

"Thank you, Simms, but this isn't really that big of a deal."

James spoke smoothly, sure to not make any part of this conversation more memorable than it already was for Simms.

The officer inserted his key into the door that read EVIDENCE in neat lettering on the frosted glass window, and pushed it open to reveal the room of shelves full of boxes and nothing else.

"You guys take your time, and let me know if you need to check anything out," Simms said, grinning as James and Danny stepped into the room. Simms closed the door, but did not lock it, his footsteps promptly going back down the hallway.

"Well, that was easy," Danny said.

"I told you it would be. We just might get to take whatever we need out of here by the sounds of it. Simms is a good guy. He'll likely tell everyone that I stopped by, so the sheriff will drop by sometime soon for a visit. Let's find what we need and get out of here."

The room was fifteen feet by fifteen feet, but the complete coverage of shelves left a small pathway clearly meant for one person at a time to walk around. James went to the back wall, Danny right behind him, as he had little choice.

"The back shelf is where all the cold case evidence is kept," James explained. "We'll store anything in here for fifty years before moving it to an external storage unit. All the other shelves are more recent cases, so don't bother looking."

The boxes sat on the shelves, labels facing outward with dates scribbled on them. He only had to check a few before finding the one he needed. "Here she is," James said, pulling out the box marked with the information: Myers, Sadie / murder / 2020

"Just the one box?" Danny asked.

"Not at all, four of them." James nodded to the others next to the one he pulled, along with another along the back of the shelf, where the bigger pieces were stored. "That box against the wall is probably the one with the axe."

James placed the first box on the floor and did the same routine with the rest, filling up their small space with all the evidence from Old Lady Myers' unsolved murder. Every item was individually packaged in a plastic evidence bag, dated and signed by the officer who had checked it in.

"Huh," Danny said, pulling out a bag with a hairbrush inside and studying the label. "Looks like Deputy Lloyd checked in most of this evidence."

"That she did. I didn't want anything falling into the wrong hands, considering what we knew. Not too many people know about these boxes today."

Danny shuffled around to the larger, elongated box and shook his head. "I can't believe it," he said, reaching down with both hands open. "It's really here."

He stood up with the axe wrapped in plastic, and held it in front of him to study the wooden handle and blade up close. "It has to be this. What else could it be? The axe was her signature."

"We can take more than the axe, just to be sure. I don't know how any of this stuff works with attaching a soul to an object, so you tell me what else might make sense."

"Well, unfortunately, there are no rules to it, as far as I know. She could have attached her soul to a toothpick to make this impossible. But, she wouldn't want to make it something difficult for her to keep track of. The last thing she'd want is for it to be on something she could easily lose. That's why I believe it would be the axe—it's something that she would have thought would always be by her side."

"While that makes sense, we need to venture further into her mind. The axe seems too obvious to me. What if she presumed she would stay longer at the Myers home? That makes me think she would have attached to any object that seemed safe within the house. Hell, maybe she thought she could get away with living there forever. That's the thing about serial killers—they never expect to actually get caught."

Danny's eyebrows shot up. "Wow, Mr. Abbott, I never thought of it that way. It actually makes sense. She clearly lived in the basement and wouldn't have had a problem with her things blending in—there was a lot of shit down there."

"Just have to think like a cop," James said with a smug grin. "I still don't think it would be something completely random—it would be something that she'd connect with at some level. Maybe something that reminded her of her childhood, or her mother. Again, impossible for us to know, but it might help us in the process of elimination."

Danny nodded and put the axe aside, shifting his attention to the boxes in front of them, their task now growing more difficult by the second. James watched as the young writer sifted through books, pens, porcelain dolls, and many mementos he knew nothing about. It all looked repetitive until he saw a jewelry box.

James crouched down and picked it up. There was something about it he couldn't ignore. An energy coursed through his arms as he studied it, the rest of the world seeming to fall into the background.

While he still didn't understand how any of this supernatural business worked, an inner voice urged him to take the jewelry box, so he tucked it under his arm while Danny continued to search through the rest of the evidence. Over the next half hour, they moved things around to different boxes, eventually filling one with the things he wanted to take home for further examination.

They wrapped up and put everything else back into place before James led them out, where he had to check out the items with Simms at the front desk.

"That's a lot of stuff," Simms commented, but made no more of a fuss.

The process went as smoothly as James had expected, and they ventured back to his truck, James keeping the box, Danny taking the axe where he would stew over the best way —and time—to go about destroying it. An action that would hopefully send Amelia Doss back to her grave.

21

The hunger plagued her again. However, it wasn't the same hunger she had experienced when she was alive. No, this was different somehow. With Danny now in possession of her axe and having learned that the former sheriff and Danny were working together to thwart her, rage filled her every thought. She wanted to kill Danny and James Abbott, but they knew she was around and would undoubtedly be prepared. She'd almost cleansed the world of Danny Espinoza that night at the museum, but then that meddlesome old biddy showed up, ruining everything.

The anger filled every part of her being, vibrating it in such a way that she thought it would destroy her.

"They *will* die," Azazoth whispered. Even Azazoth's voice enraged her. She wanted to be alone with her thoughts without him sticking his dark tendrils into her mind.

She turned and glared at the shadow, his red eyes squinting at her. As she took a threatening step toward him, Azazoth bowed his head in submission and retreated. There was a time, she remembered, when killing had been fun and satisfying. Now, it was a matter of necessity. If she wanted to survive in this form long enough to rid the world of Tyler Reynolds and exact her ultimate revenge, she had no choice. Feeding was required.

The voices of the shadows filtered to the walls, drawing her out of herself. Something was happening below.

"Why did you smack your sister?" Avery asked.

"I didn't," the little boy protested.

"Wyatt Reynolds! You hit Charlotte. Now apologize!" Avery's voice raised an octave, punctuated by a threatening overtone.

"I didn't do it. The ghosts did it."

"Do you want to explain that to your father? Or should I?"

"Fine, I did it and I'm sorry."

Amelia poked her head through the ceiling in time to see little Wyatt fold his arms over his chest in defiance; a dark look on his face.

Avery's back was to Amelia. "To your sister, not to me."

With a huff, he turned to his sister. "I'm sorry I hit you, Charlotte."

Charlotte, clutching a stuffed toy, took a long look at her brother, then at her mother, then at Amelia. "Hi, Alice," she said.

Amelia pulled her head back into the attic, just in the nick of time. By the time Avery and Wyatt looked up, Amelia was gone.

"Alice was in the ceiling," Charlotte said, in a matter-of-fact tone.

There was a pause and in a shaky voice, Avery said, "Let's wash up and get downstairs. Daddy will be home soon and he's bringing dinner."

From the attic, Amelia listened to the bustle and the foot-falls as Avery herded the children downstairs. It was time for Amelia to start her evening, and she knew just where to start it. She turned toward the vent to find Azazoth hovering behind her. "Gather the shadows," she told him. "We're going out to eat."

If it weren't that mortals couldn't hear the shadows, Amelia was convinced her posse would have sounded like a thousand mad people charging down the streets of Ridgeway in search of someone to lynch. They danced and skipped, and in excited voices whispered threats to those they passed. Even Azazoth seemed in good spirits, and this made Amelia happy. Her only friends were the shadows, and just like friends they could sometimes be aggravating, but tonight she was glad she had them. Killing alone wasn't nearly as fun. Oh, how she wished they'd seen what she'd done with the principal's body, how she'd decorated the office with his soppy entrails.

"I think it's time to paint the high school," Amelia said, with a sudden suggestion.

Azazoth's fanged grin widened. "Yes, we should paint it red."

Arm in arm, Amelia and the shadows skipped the rest of the way, like children heading to a picnic. If one listened closely, one could hear their maniacal cackles in the wind.

There were a few cars still in the parking lot. It was surprising the school hadn't closed completely with what Amelia had done to Principal Ambrose. The students were given the usual grieving time and offers of counseling, or so she'd heard. They closed the administration offices and moved them down the hall to allow the industrial cleaners space to rid the office of the murder evidence. The school had opened the following Monday and life had gone on.

That was the thing, Amelia thought, that no one really thought about. How life went on after someone died, and how easily the dead were forgotten.

The school doors were locked and inside, security

patrolled the halls. It seemed the new sheriff wasn't taking any chances. Amelia narrowed her eyes.

"Should we kill them?" one shadow asked.

Amelia looked at Azazoth with a smile and gave him a single nod.

"Kill them all," he told the shadows.

Like a mass of writhing snakes, the shadows slid under a closed door, for they only needed a tiny crack or crevice, and entered the building, coalescing into that same mass on the other side. Azazoth and Amelia entered after them.

"And what shall you do?" Azazoth asked.

"I shall find my own victim, but you're welcome to join me," she said, linking arms with Azazoth.

Together they roamed the hallways, ignoring the commotion and screams they heard along the way, until they reached the math wing of the building. Amelia stopped dead in her tracks and solidified herself. Azazoth followed suit. "What is it?" he asked.

"Mathematics," she said with a great deal of disdain. Even the word left a bad taste in her mouth. Mathematics had been her worst subject in the schoolhouse, for the short time she'd been allowed to go before woman's work kept her home cooking, bearing babies, and doing laundry. All she had to do was glance at Azazoth and he knew everything she was feeling.

They proceeded with caution, Amelia taking the lead, with Azazoth barely a step behind her. A single light in a classroom at the end of the hall was on. On the door was written a single word. *Algebra.* The two exchanged glances, and Azazoth nodded, producing something from within the dark cloak he'd manifested with. It was a six-inch hunting knife, razor sharp, with a black handle. He handed it to Amelia.

Her smile broadened and for the first time in more than a

week, she felt joy again.

"We're going to kill the teacher," Azazoth said in a sing-song voice. But instead of sounding child-like and innocent, it grated against the empty hallway and sounded more like an hungry animal panting.

Amelia giggled, and together they moved toward the classroom. As they got closer, the door swung open and a man in tan trousers and blue checked shirt stepped out, his eyes trained on Amelia. "What are you two..." his voice trailed off when he saw Azazoth. "You think this is funny, son? Halloween isn't for a few weeks." Then he noticed the knife in Amelia's hand.

She leapt forward, stabbing the man once in the stomach before stepping back. It was Azazoth's turn. He didn't need a knife at all. His razor-sharp teeth sliced into the sagging flesh of the balding man's neck as he struggled to fight back. When Azazoth pulled back, half the man's neck came with it, and blood sprayed from the vicious wound with each pump of the man's heart. He collapsed to the floor. Amelia dropped the knife into the growing pool of blood and dipped her hands into it, moving along the hallway, creating oddly satisfying bloody handprints on each of the lockers. When she needed more blood, she went back.

Azazoth took a different approach. He, too, dipped his taloned hands into the blood, but he walked along the ceiling, leaving animal-like claw prints in his wake. They did their best to drench the classroom door in blood, and when they finished, fed on what remained. By the time they heard the sirens in the distance, perhaps called to the scene by a lucky survivor, they'd finished their work. Together, they shifted from physical form and slipped into a dark closet to watch and enjoy their handiwork from a crack in the door.

It took a few minutes, but finally, the lights switched. There was a cacophony of footfalls and they stopped short.

"Holy Mary, Mother of God," one of the deputies said.

"We'd better alert the sheriff," another whispered. Then there was a loud beep. "One-four-one-nine, we have a victim in the east wing."

"Good God," the other man said, then grabbed his stomach, ran to a trash can , and retched into it.

"Who did this?" The second deputy pointed to Azazoth's tracks on the ceiling.

Both Amelia and Azazoth stifled their laughter.

"They took their time," the second deputy said.

His partner threw up in the trash can again.

"This is boring. Let's go see what havoc our friends have wrought," Azazoth said.

Amelia nodded. This wasn't quite the reaction she'd been hoping for. She'd hoped for more horror and fear, and the deputies, probably having seen more death than the average person, only displayed disgust and resignation.

It was easy to slip from the closet and slither back the way they'd come in the crevice where the floor met the wall. The path took them under an outcropping of lockers and back into a dimly lit corridor. The deputies who passed them didn't even notice. It was good to be a shadow.

When they finally made it back to the main hallway, a security guard, still alive, was being loaded onto a gurney. "It was like a thousand bees buzzing and my hands went right through them! Right through them!" he said repeatedly.

The deputies just shook their heads as the EMTs rolled him away.

"Poor bastard," the taller deputy said.

"So what do you think happened?" the short one asked.

The other shook his head. "I don't know, but it's a bloodbath. Four victims and only one survived, and he thinks it was bees."

"Must have been some big fucking bees," the short one

said.

The tall one laughed and shook his head. "I think what we have here is a gang of sick fucks, or a serial killer."

The shorter one nodded slowly.

Truly bored now, Amelia and Azazoth drifted out the open door unnoticed and rejoined their friends on a dark corner of lawn, just outside the reaches of the parking lot lights. Looking around, she noticed how healthy and vibrant her friends all looked now that they'd fed. Even Azazoth appeared more striking, his color black as pitch now instead of that blackish-gray pallor he took on when he hadn't eaten in a while. She imagined her own physical form had rejuvenated as well. Her skin firm and tight, her youth perpetual. This pleased her.

"What shall we do now?" she asked them. They'd been having such fun; it seemed a shame that the evening should end with a single massacre.

"We could deal with Ridgeway's drunkard and homeless population," Azazoth suggested dryly.

Amelia giggled. "We'd be doing this old town a favor, ridding them of the scourge."

"Yes," the rest of her friends hissed.

Ignoring the steady stream of sirens and traffic heading into the high school, they set off toward the center of Ridgeway, their dark eyes searching out vagrants and drunkards. Amelia spotted a small cache of individuals in an alley between the bar and the hardware store, hidden by dumpsters fetid with rats.

She lifted a ghostly hand. "I think I've found the party," she said. Her shadow friends congregated around her. Amelia pointed at the unfortunate souls in the alley.

As the shadows all swept into the alleyway in a swarm of darkness, all Amelia could think was that it was more fun to kill with the help of one's friends.

22

Tyler had received the phone call shortly after dinner the night before. School would be closed for at least the next week, if not indefinitely. The call came from the assistant principal, a woman by the name of Melanie Rogen. She didn't have the full story at the time, but was still in tears, as they confirmed at least two faculty members had been killed, possibly more. The police had barricaded the school grounds, and no one was allowed in or out of the building as they swept the entire school. They'd later found three dead vagrants in town. Amelia had certainly gone on a killing spree, but with the number of dead, must have had help.

Tyler's evening promptly shifted to a dark mood as he tried to figure out what to do next. There was no point in denying the truth anymore. Amelia Doss was back in Ridgeway and responsible for everything that had unfolded over the past few weeks. The kids were upstairs playing in their room when he received the call, so he told Avery what had happened.

"What the hell are we supposed to do?" she asked.

"I think it's time for you and the kids to leave here," Tyler said, sitting at the kitchen table while Avery stood, leaning against the counter.

"Leave?! Without you? You must be out of your mind."

"Not far. Remember, she's here for me. I want you to stay with my parents until this blows over."

"Tyler, this is a serial killer on the loose. It's not something that will just go away. I am *not* leaving you alone in this house."

Tyler heard the anger rising within her voice, but he stayed calm, his mind too flustered to let any emotion get the best of him. "I'm sorry, but you have to trust me. If we all stay, then we're all in danger. I'd rather it just be me at risk. Do you really expect the kids to fend for themselves if something were to happen? You can all sleep together in the guest room at my parents' house—there's plenty of room."

"Ty, listen to yourself. You want to be alone in this house to fight off a supernatural serial killer. By *yourself*. What kind of wife would I be if I just agreed to that? At least let me stay with you. The kids will be fine with your parents."

"Avery, I love you, but I just can't allow it. If things turn south, one of us needs to still be here for the kids."

Tears ran down Avery's cheeks. She rubbed her eyes and shook her head, staring at the ground. "Why is this happening? I don't understand. What did we do to deserve this? This could have been anyone else's problem, but somehow it's ours."

"I wish I had an answer for that. But it is our problem, and I plan on solving it. Danny and Sheriff Abbott have been at work—I understand they're close to a breakthrough."

"But what if they're not? Have you stopped to consider that it may not work?"

"Of course. I think about that every day, but we have to

trust in something. And if it doesn't work, we've fought her off before, and can do it again."

"And what about when you sleep? You're just going to trust that Amelia Doss will let you get your beauty rest and not disturb you?"

"I'm not going to sleep, and I'm not staying here. I'm going to Danny's and we won't stop until this is resolved. Now, go pack a bag for all three of you. We can take this one day at a time."

"Days?! Ty, I'm not going to make it. I'll go crazy sitting around, waiting to hear from you, trying to not think of the worst."

"I wish I could guarantee everything will be fine, but you know I can't do that. I can promise, however, that I will do everything I can to make sure all of us stay safe. My mom has had the house equipped and ready for this moment ever since she survived Amelia. It may be the safest place for you to be during all of this. The end is near."

"How can you possibly know that?"

"Because this is the same pattern she followed last time. It's all familiar. Now she's in my school again—I'm next on her checklist."

The truth that Tyler would never speak was that next on Amelia's checklist would be someone close to him. That's really why he wanted his wife and kids out of the house. Amelia would show up soon enough to make her next move, and if they weren't there, just maybe she'd forget about it and move in on Tyler. Or perhaps turn her attention to Danny, someone else who was equally prepared to counterattack.

Avery let more tears fall as she shrugged. "I guess all I can do is trust you. This isn't going to be easy."

"I know. And you have my word that we'll work as quickly as we can. We can't afford to drag this out any longer than it needs to be. There will only be more bodies if we do. Let me help you get the kids and their things together."

Avery lunged into Tyler's embrace, burying her face for a moment, the moisture from her face seeping through his t-shirt, and rubbed his wife's back in a gesture of ineffective comfort. The scent of the burgers they had for dinner still lingered in the kitchen, the smell making Tyler nauseous as his mind raced for what awaited once Avery and the kids left.

"I love you," Avery said as she pulled her head off his chest, her watery eyes falling upon his. "You *have* to make it out of this alive."

Tyler nodded. "I will. This isn't how it ends."

Avery wiped her face clear before turning and heading up the stairs, where she would spend the next fifteen minutes getting a bag together. Tyler followed and did the same for the kids, talking to them while Wyatt played with toy dinosaurs, and Charlotte dressed up as a princess, dancing in front of the mirror to the soft tunes of Radio Disney.

"Are we going somewhere, Daddy?" Wyatt asked once he realized Tyler was packing their clothes into a duffel bag.

"Yeah, buddy. You guys are going with Mommy to Grandma and Grandpa's house for a couple of nights. I have to do some work around the house, and it might be too noisy for you all to sleep."

"Yay!" Charlotte cried, jumping up and down. "Gramma! Grampa!"

Wyatt couldn't resist the satisfaction, either, a wide grin taking control of his face. Like most young children with grandparents in town, they loved when they got to visit a place with lax rules and a questionable amount of sugary snacks. Normally, Tyler would have to brace himself for the tornadoes his children became in the presence of his parents, but under the circumstances, he couldn't think of anything better for them to keep their minds distracted while he and Danny battled with a demon.

Once everything was together, Tyler saw them out, kissing his kids on the forehead before they buckled into their carseats, and sharing a long, dramatic kiss with his wife. While he embraced the possibility of never seeing them again, Tyler's instinct insisted that he would. Avery pulled the car out of the driveway, the evening already dark as the headlights blinded him before she turned away and vanished from the neighborhood.

Tyler wasted no time hopping into his car and firing up the engine. He didn't need to bring anything with him; he just needed to get to Danny's house, where they would hopefully end this thing within the next twenty-four hours. While he didn't expect it to go so smoothly, he clung to his optimism.

It only took him ten minutes to race across town, devoid of traffic as most of the town shutdown early on weeknights. In the night, Danny's house looked haunted, a lone light flickering on the front porch, a massive window looking into the living room emitting a soft glow of yellow light.

My friend, the crazy horror writer, Tyler thought, letting out a nervous chuckle as he parked and immediately hopped out of the car and hurried to the door. He knocked and looked around, the darkness of the woods swallowing him, not a neighbor in sight. Just the way Danny liked it.

The door swung open, Danny appearing with his hair in a frazzled mess, his eyes bloodshot.

"What's wrong?" Danny asked, his voice desperate and dripping with panic.

"You hear about the murders at the school and in town?" Tyler asked.

"No—I've been trying to figure out this chant and the best way to do it. I think it's about ready. Come in." Tyler entered, and Danny closed the door behind him, bolting the lock, something he never did. "There were more murders?"

"Yes. I'm not even sure of all the details. I got a call from the assistant principal saying they found multiple faculty members murdered. Didn't say who, or how, but I think we know the answer to the second question."

"Absolutely. So why are you here?"

"It's time, Dan. Whatever you've been working on, we need to do it tonight. I sent Avery and the kids to my parents' house. It's just not safe anymore. If we let Amelia live another day, I'm not sure the rest of us will make it."

Danny nodded and shuffled away from the front door into his living room, where a long axe lay on the coffee table.

"Holy shit!" Tyler gasped. "Is that what I think it is?"

"Yes. Mr. Abbott got us into that evidence room, and even had us take a box of evidence out. He has the box, but I have the axe. He knows what's going on."

Tyler looked around for clues, but saw nothing else besides an open book on the couch, boxes of long text filling the entirety of the visible pages. "What *is* going on?"

"I told you, I think Amelia attached her soul to an object. I'm certain it's this axe. It's the one she used fifteen years ago —taken from the Myers basement. If we destroy it successfully, we can finally get rid of her. But it all has to be *perfect*."

Danny spoke at a rapid rate Tyler had never heard from his best friend of over two decades. "What can I do to help?" he asked.

"Not much at this point. I've spent all day practicing. The timing has to be right, the cadence has to be precise."

"I thought you said we just have to destroy it. Why don't we just cut it in half with a saw?"

Danny shook his head violently. "It's not like that. We have to destroy it, but it's all part of a process. Like I said, there is a specific timing and flow to this. It all has to hit together in sync. Trust me!" Tyler took a step back as Danny lunged forward and grabbed the axe, hoisting it in the air and turning it so the handle stuck out to Tyler. "Grab it. And tell me if I'm wrong. But I've felt a weird energy from this axe all day long."

Tyler frowned as his eyes fell upon the handle, studying the weapon that had taken so many lives. A weapon that was, he supposed, meant to take his life. He reached out with both hands and wrapped his fingers around the smooth wooden handle. He had expected a mystical jolt of sorts upon making contact, but nothing happened. Danny let go and allowed the weight to fall entirely into Tyler's grip.

"It feels like an axe," Tyler said, not sure what he was supposed to experience. "A regular axe, nothing different from the one in my shed."

Danny tossed his hands up, his eyes crazed as they remained glued to the axe. "I know what I've felt all day—no mistaking it. There is an intense energy coming from that axe. It has to be her soul."

While Tyler felt nothing of the sorts, he still grew uncomfortable by simply holding the axe. He shuffled forward and placed the murder weapon back on the coffee table. "Look, Dan, I don't know about any of this stuff, but it seems you have it under control. I'll be here for support, just let me know if I can help."

Danny smirked as he stepped up to the table and retrieved the axe. "Let's go to her grave. Get Mr. Abbott on the phone."

❧ 23 ☙

Danny held the axe in his gloved hands and shuddered. This was the same axe Amelia Doss had used numerous Ridgeway and Denver citizens. He gulped.

James Abbott narrowed his eyes. "You all right there, Espinoza?"

"Yes, sir," Danny said almost reflexively. Since they were going to destroy the axe, James insisted Danny didn't need to wear the latex gloves, but the mere thought of touching the dried blood that had soaked into the wood gave him the willies.

"You know what you're doing, then?" Abbott asked.

He merely nodded and glanced at Tyler, who'd been quiet this whole time. Danny had wanted to ask James what Rachel Lloyd would think about him taking the axe, but he thought better of it. It was none of his business.

All Danny wanted was to get the ritual over with. "So should we destroy the axe first and then perform the exorcism?" He didn't know why he asked them, because he already knew that he wanted to destroy the axe first. He'd wrestled with this choice for a few days now, even after the terrifying run-in with Amelia's ghost at the museum.

Tyler nodded once. "Axe."

"I don't care. Let's get this show on the road, gentlemen. I'd rather not be stuck out here all night." James looked up at the clear night sky. While days in the Colorado mountains could be quite comfortable, it got chilly at night. His eyes moved back to the pit they'd dug to burn the axe in. They had to be careful they didn't start a forest fire and with that in mind, there were two full fire extinguishers standing at James' feet.

Before them, the grave of Amelia Doss, its damaged headstone rife with graffiti, beckoned. Danny set the axe on the ground and began visualizing the tether that connected the axe to Amelia. It was easy to visualize Amelia. Her image had been burned into his brain since the first day he saw her. The sight of her, even in his mind's eye, sent a chill up his spine. He focused and took out the bag of black poppy seeds, pepper, and henbane from his jacket pocket and poured it over and around the axe, visualizing the invisible tether losing its strength. While he worried the simple act of visualizing Amelia would draw her to them, he tried not to think about that. Instead, he focused on the herbs, how their power would dissolve the cord. Finally, he doused the axe with a small amount of diesel fuel, lit a piece of newspaper, then held that against the diesel-soaked axe until the fire sparked. It took longer than he expected.

"Should have let me bring the blowtorch," James said.

Tyler fought back a nervous laugh.

Danny ignored them, holding his hands two feet above the pit, visualizing the flames destroying both the axe and what remained of its tether to Amelia Doss. If she was attached to the axe, she wouldn't be for long. In his mind's eye, the flames lifted higher and higher. The heat from the flame was enough to ignite the axe handle and incinerate it. While the head of the axe would remain, they could bury it there, alongside Amelia Doss.

"Danny!" Tyler cried out.

A hand reached out and yanked Danny by the jacket. He stumbled backward, his eyes now open, staring at the eerily high white flame. Danny turned to find James standing next to him, his hand still on Danny's jacket.

He let go. "You need to watch yourself, son."

Danny just nodded, noticing Tyler's sigh of relief.

Tyler turned to him. "Is it done? Don't you have to say the magic words or something?"

He shook his head. "Magic is more about intent and visualization accompanied by tangible, meaningful actions." These were Lavinia's words, but they certainly sounded authoritative coming from his lips. His eyes met Tyler's then. "The exorcism, however..."

"I still think that's ridiculous." Tyler shrugged. "I mean, I'm not possessed."

Even James wasn't taking Tyler's word for it. "What can it hurt?"

"Fine. I get it." Tyler shook his head.

Then, without provocation, the flame danced skyward in a long spiral, then dropped to nothing and extinguished. Danny put one hand on his chest as if that would stop his heart from beating through his rib cage.

The ex-sheriff flicked on his flashlight and shined it into the now-black hole. There was nothing left of the axe except a pile of ash and the metal head covered with thick, black soot. James reached down and picked up the small shovel they'd brought, and handed it to Danny. "Cover it up." His tone hinted at finality.

Danny only hoped James was right. He scooped the hill of dirt back into the hole, covering the head of the axe and the ash from its handle until the earth was flat again. He banged the back of the shovel over the spot to pack it down.

"Okay, so where do you want me?" Tyler asked. It was obvious he was just going along with it to pacify Danny, and James. Tyler wasn't religious by any means, but then, neither was Danny.

"Right where you are is fine. First, I'll sprinkle you with holy water, anoint you with holy oil, and I'll have to read the incantation while visualizing all bad spirits within you vanishing and being chased away."

Tyler smirked.

"Be serious, Ty."

This time, Tyler laughed. "I'm sorry. I'm trying to be serious, it's just, if I was possessed, you'd think I would know it. That's all. Because if you think about it, I'd have to have been possessed for the last sixteen years."

James let out an exasperated sigh. "Let's get on with it."

Danny wanted to ask if he was keeping the two of from something more important, but he refrained. He didn't expect them to understand the intricacies of magic and spirit work, not that he fully understood it himself. He had, however, had enough conversations with Lavinia and attended enough of her workshops to know it was as real as Amelia Doss coming back from the dead. He removed the bottle of holy water from his jacket, opened it, took a sniff just to be sure he'd grabbed the right bottle, and splashed Tyler with it.

Tyler wiped his face. "You could have given me some warning!"

Danny ignored this, imagining Tyler surrounded by a bright white light. He removed the small dram vial of oil from his pocket, put a dab on his finger, and smudged it on Tyler's forehead, still visualizing the holy light. He began the incantation that Lavinia had given him and that he'd been practicing: *"Regna terrae, cantata Deo, psallite Cernunnos, Regna terrae, cantata Dea psallite Aradia. caeli Deus, Deus terrae, Humiliter majestati gloriae tuae supplicamus Ut ab omni infernalium spirituum potestate, Laqueo, and deceptione nequitia, Omnis fallaciae, libera nos, dominates. Exorcizamus you omnis immundus spiritus Omnis satanica potestas, omnis incursio, Infernalis adversarii, omnis legio, Omnis and congregatio secta diabolica. Ab insidiis diaboli, libera nos, dominates, Ut coven tuam secura tibi libertate servire facias, Te rogamus, audi nos! Ut inimicos sanctae circulae humiliare digneris, Te rogamus, audi nos! Terribilis Deus Sanctuario suo, Cernunnos ipse truderit virtutem plebi Suae, Aradia ipse fortitudinem plebi Suae. Benedictus Deus, Gloria Patri, Benedictus Dea, Matri gloria!"*

Which, roughly translated, meant:

The kingdoms of the earth, enchanted to God, sing praise to Cernunnos, the Kingdoms of the earth, the enchanted Goddess with Aradia, the sky God, God of the earth, humble majesty of your glory. Deliver us from all infernal spirits that control, snare, and corrupt with their wickedness. Deliver us from the illusions that dominate us. Exorcise every unclean spirit, every Satanic power, every invasion, infernal opponent, every legion, and all things diabolical. From the snares of the Devil, deliver us. We secure his freedom; we ask You, hear us! To the enemies of the holy circulae thou wouldst vouch safety to the humble, we ask You, hear us! Awesome God, in the sanctuary of Cernunnos, he brings power to his own. By Aradia bring strength to his own. Blessed be God, Glory be to the Father, Blessed Goddess, the Mother of glory!

As he said the incantation, he felt the power in his words build, rising higher and higher into the crisp night air until something in the ether seemed to snap. And the incantation was finished and a powerful wave of calm and peace fell over them. Tyler and James must have felt it, too, judging by the surprised looks on their faces.

"Did you feel that?" Danny asked.

Tyler, who appeared shaky, nodded. "Yeah. That was weird."

"Maybe he was possessed after all," James whispered. "Are we done here? Do you have to bless or burn anything else?" His eyes darted around the clearing as if he expected hellfire to rain down on them any moment.

But everything was calm. The air was lighter, and Danny felt immensely better. "That was it. We can go."

"Let's do it then. Grab our gear, men." James held the flashlight for them while Danny and Tyler picked up the shovel and fire extinguishers. Danny secured the empty bottles of diesel and holy water in his pocket. He still had the holy oil, and the empty plastic bag the herbs had been in. Together, they made their way back down the trail to their vehicles near the road. There, James got into his truck, and Danny and Tyler into Tyler's car. They followed the ex-sheriff onto the county road and back toward the Ridgeway town center.

Tyler didn't say anything, just kept his eyes on the road and both hands on the wheel.

"That went smoother than I expected," Danny said, hoping to spark a conversation. He hated long silences.

"But, do you think it worked? Because we are talking about my life here." Tyler said this in all seriousness. But after a few moments, his grim expression gave way to a smile. "I'm messing with you, Dan."

"How can you be so..." He let the sentence trail off into silence.

Tyler turned serious again. "I'm scared shitless that it won't work. She's come back twice after these rituals of yours. But I can't let the threat of Amelia Doss keep me from living and having a sense of humor." He let out a long exhale.

Danny didn't know how his best friend did it. One intimate run-in with Amelia at the museum had been enough for him, personally. She'd almost got him with that pitchfork. His left hand traveled up to his right bicep where he'd been grazed by one of the tines and he rubbed it, even though it didn't hurt.

"Should we listen to the radio?" Tyler glanced over at him.

"Yeah, sure," Danny said.

Tyler turned on the radio and set the volume low. "How long do you think it will take before we know if this worked or not?"

He shrugged. "I don't know. Um, I'd say if we haven't seen any sign of her in a week or two, we can be relatively certain we got rid of her this time?"

"Or at least for another fifteen years," Tyler said. The light from the street lamps swept across Tyler's face, and for the first time Danny realized just how much older they were. Even though it didn't feel like it, they were no longer young kids.

"Let's hope it's for good. I don't want to do this again in our fifties."

Tyler chuckled. "You and me both. But hey, chin up Danny. You got rid of her for fifteen years last time. It keeps improving each time you do one of your rituals, right? It's only a matter of time before she really leaves."

Danny wasn't nearly as optimistic, but he forced a smile anyway. "Yeah. That's true." Something in his gut, however, told him to not get comfortable until they knew for sure that Amelia Doss was gone for good.

24

A melia had followed them up to the Doss family plot and hid in the shadows while Tyler, Danny, and the lawman dug a wide hole at the base of her grave.

"What do you think they're doing?" Azazoth asked, a hint of sarcasm in his voice.

She turned to her shadow friend. "Another ritual, I suppose." While the prospect of another ritual should have worried her, since the last one had thrown her into a stasis for fifteen years, Danny's haphazard magic didn't scare her. She'd heard Danny talking to someone on the phone about exorcism and bound objects. The only reason she'd even bothered to follow them here was because the old lawman, James Abbott, had reacquired her axe. She hadn't known where it was, and now she knew the sheriff had it stowed away in something called an evidence locker. But now there was the possibility of getting her axe back. The axe was like an old friend, calling to her.

"You don't need the axe," Azazoth whispered over her shoulder.

She didn't answer him. Of course she didn't need the axe,

she was simply fond of it. After all, she'd killed so many filthy souls with that axe. Letting out a wistful sigh, she watched with great interest. Maybe a small part of her was a little worried about Danny's sorcery, and naturally she wanted to make sure they would not try to send her away again.

When Danny pulled out the axe and held it in front of him, she thought about storming in as a cold wind and yanking it from his mortal hands, but she felt Azazoth's embrace holding her back.

"You no longer have need of such weapons," he repeated.

Amelia was wondering if Azazoth was more of a hindrance than a helper. She turned her head and glared at him. He was right, of course. She didn't need an axe when she could manifest her fingers into knives. Her new form was stronger and more versatile. Still, she hated Azazoth was right and that he frequently pointed out all the things she was wrong about.

Danny dropped the axe into the hole.

Amelia lifted an ethereal eyebrow from her hiding place in the tenebrous forest foliage less than ten yards away. Then she watched as they burned the axe and buried what remained.

It made no sense.

"They think you're connected to that axe, or Tyler. So by severing those connections, they think you'll disappear," Azazoth clarified.

Once again, she didn't respond to her friend. He was such a know-it-all.

They remained in their hiding spot amid the trees while Danny performed a rather lively exorcism, the words chilling Amelia a bit. There was something striking and threatening about them. Something she didn't like, and it had put her off of continuing to watch them. She turned to where Azazoth had been only moments before, but he was gone. He'd likely gone to convene with the other shadows up at the mine. As Tyler and his posse left, she turned in the opposite direction and made her way up to the mine, no longer amused or feeling like she had the upper hand.

She wasn't even sure she wanted to join her friends. There was no cause for celebration because Tyler wasn't dead yet. She hadn't settled the score. Finding a secluded outcropping of rock further up the mountain, she perched on top of it and looked out over Ridgeway, the light pollution from the growing town a blinding eyesore of everything that was unholy in this world.

One question settled in Amelia's mind. What did Tyler Reynolds care about most? He'd come after his own mother, but whether he would have sacrificed himself for her was doubtful. One of his own children, however... But which one? Did it matter? Would a father sacrifice himself to save his offspring?

A slow smile spread over her lips, and her sullen disposition faded. Yes. Now it was just a matter of getting her friends on board so they could help her with the next phase of her plan. By the end of the week, Tyler Reynolds would be dead and she could finally rest.

With a flourish, she turned into a wisp of smoke and drifted down the mountain, riding the air current like white water rapids, enjoying the rush flying gave her. When she reached the opening of the mine, she willed herself solid and stepped into the entrance.

Inside, the worried whispers of the shadows filled her ears.

"What's wrong with him?" one asked.

"I think he's dying," another said.

Amelia shoved her way through the shadows, down the long tunnel and into the clearing where the tunnel broke off into more tunnels. There, in a heap on the floor, Azazoth's form lay unmoving, his red piercing eyes parted ever so slightly and his forked tongue hanging out between razor-sharp teeth.

She kneeled next to him and shook him vigorously by the shoulder. "Azazoth, get up. This is no time to mess around."

The onlooking shadows tittered.

Azazoth barely moved, his now solid form reeking of sulfur.

This wasn't Amelia's problem. While she could have certainly used Azazoth's help in finishing up what she'd started, he wasn't necessary. A casualty for her cause.

Amelia stood and addressed the only ones who'd ever talked to her and cared for her. "Azazoth is dead. It is best we leave him to the cave. He was a brave fighter for the cause." Then she turned and saluted him as if she were a tin soldier saluting a fallen brother.

The shadows lined up on either side of her and followed suit.

"Azazoth is dead," some of them whispered. "Dead."

It was a shame, really. With those gleaming fangs and spooky red eyes, he was rather impressive. But perhaps it was better that he was dead. She didn't spend too much time ruminating over how he might have died, but she had noticed that sometimes shadows merely fell and the others left them to decay and disappear. They came and went, and she wasn't sure if the surrounding shadows now were the ones who'd been around her when she was alive. They didn't have names, usually. Azazoth had been the first.

Again, it was better that he was dead because he scared children, and the next part of her plan depended on her taking one of the Reynolds children. She'd always been good with children on her own. They trusted her. They followed her.

"Sleep well, Azazoth!" She turned away from her friend's

body and left the cave, her delight in the plan undiminished. The other shadows followed her out in single file, like a funeral procession. Once they were outside the cave again, Amelia turned to address them. "First, we feast on the animals of the forest, then we return to the Reynolds house, but we must be silent. After all, I need to make friends."

They supped on venison and muskrat and when they finished, returned to the Reynolds house, but no one was there. She could tell Avery and Tyler had been arguing again. There was a tension in the air. Tension had a certain vibration to it, and ever since she'd shed her physical form, she could feel those vibrations more acutely. With no one home, she moved through the walls, being as quiet as she could manage, and emerged into the children's closet. She peeked out the crack. The room was empty. Where were they?

A flash of insight told her exactly where. Tyler's childhood home. A wicked grin crossed her lips, and she left the house, and minutes later, found herself in Tyler's parents' house. While the house was silent, she could feel them. She made her way up to Tyler's childhood bedroom and slipped into the closet, opening it just a crack. There they were. Wyatt and Charlotte were sound asleep in the shared bed.

Amelia closed her eyes and visualized herself as a child, and when she felt her body turn solid, she looked down at herself in the darkness. While human eyes did not see so well in the darkness, Amelia had adjusted and could see everything. She looked perfect. Perfect enough to convince Charlotte Reynolds that she was Alice. She poked her head out of the closet and looked around the dimly lit room. From the ceiling, stars with an eerie green glow looked down on them. Amelia didn't dare scare the children by startling them awake. Besides, she only wanted to talk to the younger one. The three-year-old was far more impressionable and undoubtedly more trusting than her older brother.

It took about fifteen minutes of intense staring, but the child's reflexes finally kicked in and Charlotte woke and sat straight up, her eyes on Amelia. Amelia put a child-sized finger to her lips, then gave Charlotte a wide, innocent smile and held out her hand.

Charlotte, with a doll in hand, slid out of her small bed, glanced back at her brother, but took Amelia's hand and followed her from the bedroom. They crept through the hallway, careful to not wake the child's mother, who slept in a spare bedroom, and Tyler's parents, and down the stairs, into the empty family room.

"We can't be out of bed. We'll get in trouble," Charlotte protested in a whisper.

"It's okay," Amelia said. "I thought we could play down here."

"Where do you live?"

"In the walls. Do you remember who I am?" Amelia plopped herself down on the rug and took a ball from next to the coffee table and started rolling it on the floor.

Charlotte watched with some suspicion, but then settled and sat down beside her. "I know—you're Alice. But you live at *my* house."

Amelia nodded. "I live in all the houses," she explained. "We can be good friends. I don't have a sister."

"Me neither."

"Brothers are a pain," Amelia told her.

Charlotte nodded emphatically.

There was a brief noise upstairs, and they both turned toward the staircase. Amelia put her finger to her lips.

The sullen three-year-old's serious expression broke into a grin. "We have to be quiet," Amelia whispered.

This would not be easy, since a three-year-old's idea of quiet was anything but. God, she disliked children. She hadn't even liked her own very much. The thought of killing the child had crossed her mind, but this time around, she didn't have time to waste. Now that Tyler, Danny, and the ex-sheriff were onto her, she had to hurry. Killing her would only give Tyler and Danny more reason to try more rituals, and it was quite possible one of them would work.

She leaned toward the child. "Let's not tell anyone we're friends. Not your brother or your parents."

"Why?"

Amelia fought back an exasperated sigh. Children were always full of questions, and if she wanted to placate Charlotte and get her to believe she was just another child, there was no room for error. "Because they won't understand and will just get mad."

"Why?" Charlotte asked again.

"Because only you can see me. They'll think you're just making me up." Amelia shrugged her shoulders. "Let's play hide-and-go-seek. That's a quiet game. Who is going to count?"

Charlotte considered this for a moment, her tousled head of hair tipping to one side in thought. "I don't know how."

Amelia nodded. "Okay. I'll count, and you hide."

With a nod of agreement, Charlotte waited until Amelia turned away, then scurried off to find a good hiding spot.

Amelia counted ever so quietly, waiting for the soft patter of sock-clad feet to go silent. She heard a door in the kitchen close. The child was hiding in the pantry. "Ready or not, here I come," she whispered.

Then she heard footfalls on the staircase. Amelia willed herself back into her shadow form and dove beneath the couch.

Tyler's mother stepped into the room and looked around, glancing at the corner lamp they kept on at night. "Charlotte?"

A faint giggle emerged from the kitchen and the grandmother, much older now than when Amelia had kidnapped her, turned toward the noise. Her eyes widened, and she visibly swallowed.

A sly grin slid over Amelia's shadow lips. She watched, following at a safe distance and keeping to the shadows, as Wendy Reynolds entered the kitchen and flicked on the light. "Charlotte?"

No answer.

She reached out, hesitated, but took the door and opened it, a flood of relief washing over her face. "What are you doing in the pantry? It's three in the morning."

Charlotte looked around. "I want a snack."

Smart little thing, Amelia thought. Even three-year-olds lied.

"Well, you can have one glass of milk and a single cookie, but don't tell your mother. Then we'll go back to bed." She shook her head with a smile. "Come on."

Amelia knew then that she couldn't wait any longer. Even Wendy Reynolds was suspicious, and the second Charlotte started talking about her friend Alice, the jig was up.

25

Tyler woke the next morning on Danny's living room couch, the sun streaming through the front curtains. He had opted to spend the night at Danny's place instead of being alone in his abandoned house. The night had passed with plenty of tossing and turning, both from anxiety and excitement. Could this finally be the day he woke up and didn't have to worry about Amelia, hacking away at the back of his mind as she had done for the past fifteen years? He didn't think so. As intense as last night's rituals had been, a voice deep down within Tyler suggested none of it worked. His gut instinct told him to stay alert and be ready for a most ferocious counterattack by Amelia Doss.

There should have been more that happened. Danny performed his ritual, and they promptly hopped in the car to leave. Nobody appeared at the gravesite. No spirits screamed from the depths of hell. It had been a fairly normal weeknight in the town of Ridgeway, and that's what bothered Tyler the most as he started the new day ahead. If Amelia Doss really had been sent back to the grave, he would have known. Aside from living in his thoughts, she was very much a part of him.

A part of him that remained as Danny powered up his coffee machine in the kitchen and filled the entire house with the soothing aromas of a strong Colombian brew.

Tyler sat up, his hair smushed in different directions, flattened on the left side of his head where he had laid on the pillow all night. He stood and fastened his borrowed robe over his body and ventured into the kitchen.

Danny stood like a zombie in front of the coffee machine, eyes still bloodshot, the bags under his eyes an even darker shade as he swayed on his feet.

"Dan, are you okay?" Tyler asked, quickly moving closer to his friend.

Danny shrugged. "Got zero sleep last night. All I could do was play the ritual over in my head. I don't think it worked, Ty, but I'm not sure. Should we go back to the grave to see?"

"I don't know, man. I gotta say, I feel the same way. I don't *feel* like she's gone. Something is still off."

"Fuck!" Danny barked to the ceiling, kicking the cupboards below the countertop. "I just want this bitch gone! Why the hell did I have to bring her back?! Stupid. I wish I could go back in time and slap the shit out of myself. All this blood is on my hands, Ty. None of this would have happened if I didn't play cute with the dead."

Tyler had jumped back a step when Danny shouted, his body tensing up while his friend had a mental breakdown. "You can dwell on the past all you want, Dan, but that doesn't change anything today. I have no doubts the ritual was done properly. You spent hours obsessing over all the details. But this can only mean one thing: the axe was the wrong object."

Danny shook his head so violently Tyler thought it might fly right out the kitchen window. "It *had* to be the axe. Nothing else makes sense. There were so many little things in the boxes that she could have been tied to if it wasn't the axe. Who's to say it's even something in one of those evidence boxes? It could be a little blade of grass, floating across the mountains each time the wind blows. We're so fucked! We need to leave Ridgeway again, before anyone else gets hurt."

Danny spoke what felt like a million words per minute. Tyler kept his voice as calm as he could manage. "You said the sheriff has a box of stuff, right? Let's just call him and see if we can go over for a look. Maybe he's had a look for himself."

"Please, Ty. Mr. Abbott doesn't know anything about this stuff. He's pretty much useless outside of helping us get the axe. He still doesn't fully believe any of this is real."

"All I'm saying is perhaps an outside perspective—which he certainly has—can be helpful. You've taken on too much of this by yourself. Let us take some burden off your shoulders. At the very least, we need to make a new plan. I'll call him."

"Do whatever you think—I have to get back to figuring out where this all went wrong."

Tyler sensed a sudden shift. He now felt it was his responsibility to see this matter through its end. Danny was too exhausted to think straight, too defeated by last night's failure to function as he should. While Danny would still play a key role and handle any chants or rituals that needed to take place, Tyler would overlook the logistics of their decisions from now on.

Danny remained in front of the coffeepot, finally pouring himself a mug. Tyler stepped out of the kitchen and returned to the living room, where he had left his cell phone on the coffee table. He snatched it and quickly dialed James.

He answered, sounding full of much more energy than the two of them.

"Mr. Abbott," Tyler said, faking confidence. "How was your night?"

"It was good. Got some much needed rest. How was it for you two?"

"Neither of us slept. Today's going to be interesting because we are both fairly certain what we did last night didn't work. Amelia is still out there."

"Are you shittin' me? All that, and we made no progress?"

James fell silent, and Tyler didn't know what to say, ashamed that they had failed, unsure why he took it so personally when it had all been planned out and executed by Danny. Perhaps he had some resentment toward being used in a half-hearted exorcism.

"I think we need to come over and look through that other box of stuff you have from the evidence room," Tyler finally said.

"Afraid we can't do that today. Sheriff Lloyd is stopping by to chat. Turns out she's not so pleased I took evidence home without her approval. Now, it's nothing to worry about—she's going to let me hold on to it since the case has been cold for over a decade, but I know she's going to have a list of questions, especially with the recent murders. If she saw either of you two here, sifting through that box, then she'd definitely take it all back to the station. Trust me on this. Besides, I think I know what item that soul is attached to. You guys can plan to swing by later tonight to pick it up—I won't be going back into the woods to perform any more rituals. It felt weird, and now there are eyes on me."

How James could speak of all this so nonchalantly blew Tyler's mind. But the man was an ex-sheriff, and it took a ton to excite him.

"Wait, you think you know what Amelia's soul is attached to? What? How?"

"It's one of those jewelry boxes that plays music when you open the lid. I put the box on my kitchen counter and haven't really touched it. But the music started playing. I figured maybe the lid had opened—things moved around the box— and it *was* open. The first time. I closed it and put it underneath a porcelain doll so the lid wouldn't open again. But then the music played again later. I checked the box, and nothing had moved—the box was exactly where I left it with the lid closed. But the music kept playing. So then I figured it was just an old box—looks like it could be from the 1800s. Probably faulty and nothing to worry about. But it's kept on playing. I hear the music at least every couple hours, and it will play for a minute or two before stopping. Part of me still wants to believe that is only has some faulty parts inside, but I think I know better—knowing where it came from."

Tyler's heart drummed against his ribs. How could James still act so calmly about this? That jewelry box was definitely the answer. It might even be Amelia's original possession, from the actual life she lived over a century ago. In his early days of research, he had found it peculiar that the authorities never cleared all of Amelia's belongings from her house after her hanging. They packed up most things from the main and upper levels, but they had determined the basement to be a waste of time—the area having only been swept for potential dead bodies in hiding. If Amelia had found something that used to be hers, that would make even more sense for her wanting to attach her soul to it.

"We need to see that jewelry box," Tyler said. "You're sure we can't come any earlier than tonight?"

"Afraid so. Sheriff Lloyd told me she'd be by at some point today. Didn't clarify when. She has a lot going on with all these murders, so it's impossible for me to take any guesses. I figure it will be before nightfall, so that's why I say tonight. I also don't know how our conversation will go. Could run for quite a while if she goes on a tangent. How about I call you boys as soon as she leaves?"

"That works, thank you."

They hung up, and Tyler tossed his phone on the couch, shaking his head. They had what they needed, but had to wait for it. He checked the clock on the wall to find it was only nine o'clock. They'd have to kill the entire day before getting their next shot at sending Amelia back to the grave.

"Fuck," he muttered under his breath.

Danny was still in the kitchen, sipping from his coffee mug, gazing out the window to his backyard surrounded by tall trees. Tyler entered. "I have some good news and some bad news."

Danny spun around, the coffee providing him with just enough energy to function. "What did he say?"

"Well, the good news is he thinks—he *knows*—what we need to destroy. There is a jewelry box that plays music. He said it keeps playing no matter what he does to stop it. It's old, and I think it might be Amelia's from her original life."

"What's the bad news?"

"We have to wait until tonight to go get it. He said the sheriff is planning on stopping by his house today. She's not happy he took that stuff. He made it clear we need to stay away until he calls and confirms it's safe for us to head over."

Danny nodded. "I really thought it was the ax. I saw the jewelry box. Even considered it as a possible link for a half a second. But... sorry for screwing that up."

"Don't sweat it. I'm sure it was like picking a needle out of a haystack. The fact that we now know what it is has probably saved more lives."

"But we don't know, Ty. That's the point—we have to try this until we see her back in the ground. What if he's sure about this box like I was about the axe? We all saw how that worked out."

"Then we keep trying until it works."

Danny let out a long exhale, shaking his head. "We can't do this forever, Ty. At some point we either win, or decide to give up. I'm ready to accept that reality. Are you?"

Tyler had considered this plenty of times. What Danny

didn't realize was that he was playing a game with different stakes. In Danny's world, he could move to Hollywood and never have to deal with Amelia Doss again. For Tyler, the finish line wasn't so simple. Either he died, or Amelia died. There were no other options.

182

❧ 26 ☙

James Abbott poured his first cup of tea for the late afternoon. He had called Tyler to let him know Sheriff Lloyd had left. Tyler told him Danny would be there in ten minutes. The sheriff was nowhere near as upset as her initial text messages had seemed. In fact, she wasn't upset at all. She simply wanted to know what James was up to and if it could have any connections to the recent murders in town.

He fudged some details to keep Tyler and Danny protected, explaining that he was the one who had been spending his free time—which was plentiful—digging into the unsolved murders from fifteen years earlier. A retired cop obsessing over a cold case from earlier in their career was far from unusual, and the sheriff accepted it as plausible.

Even though Amelia Doss had been responsible for those old murders and the current ones, the last thing they needed was the police department snooping around Danny's rituals. That would unleash a flurry of questions and possibly paint Danny as a potential suspect. As much as he hated it, James had to play this close to the chest to allow the boys to end this matter with their unorthodox methods.

The sheriff had spent two hours with James, chatting about his findings, picking his brain for options regarding the new murders, and catching up.

A knock came on his door exactly ten minutes after he had called Tyler, and he took a sip of his tea before going to open it. Danny stood on the other side, a tired grin smacked across his face.

"You take a nap today?" James asked, shuffling aside to let Danny enter the house.

"Only for about forty-five minutes. My mind won't let me rest until we get this resolved."

James debated lecturing the young man about the importance of sleep to a functioning brain, but figured it would do no good at this point in time.

"Sheriff Lloyd was here?" Danny asked.

"Yep. Nothing to worry about. You boys are free to do as you please with this evidence—just make sure I have *something* to take back, at least."

Danny nodded, his eyes bouncing around the house.

"Looking for the box? I haven't touched that thing since it first started playing music. I'm more convinced now that it's what you're looking for. It started playing more often, but when Sheriff Lloyd arrived, it didn't play for the whole two hours she was here. The fact that it didn't has made me even more suspicious."

"Can I see it?"

"Come into the kitchen." James led the way, happy to grab his cup of tea he had left on the countertop, taking another sip as he pointed to the box full of junk. "Have at it. Don't mind if I never have to see it again."

James stayed back and watched as Danny sifted through the old belongings, pulling out the jewelry box and holding it high above his head to examine it.

"I'll take it tonight and try the ritual again. Are you going to hold on to the rest of that stuff for long?"

"She didn't say I had to take it back soon—if at all."

"Perfect. Thank you, Mr. Abbott. I hope this is the one that sends Amelia home." Danny tucked the jewelry box under his arm and moved toward the front door.

"Good luck tonight, and stay safe. I'll stay by my phone in case you need to call for anything. Don't hesitate."

Danny nodded and let himself out. James bolted the lock on his door and watched through the window as Danny pulled out of the driveway. James couldn't recall a time he had ever seen a man so exhausted. He could only hope it wouldn't alter his ability to perform whatever dark magic he needed to do in the woods.

The sun had already set, and he suspected Danny would head straight to the gravesite with the jewelry box.

Just as James turned around, glass shattered in the kitchen, causing him to jump back. "What the hell?"

He hurried into the kitchen to find his cup of tea on the floor, the ceramic shards splattered in every direction, the liquid puddling at the foot of the counters. "Did I leave it on the edge?" he asked, thinking back, unsure where he had placed it down. He had been so focused on Danny that it was entirely possible he hadn't been paying attention. Nothing else was out of place, so he accepted this as his own mistake.

With a grumble, James ripped a strip of paper towel off the spool and mopped up the tea, pushing the chunks of ceramic into a pile until he could grab the broom and dust-pan. Just as he tossed the soaked paper towels in the trash can, footsteps rumbled across the living room behind him.

James spun around, his hand immediately shooting to his hip, where he normally kept his pistol. But being home, he had left it on the nightstand in his bedroom. He scanned the kitchen, opting for a chef's knife in the knife rack on the counter.

"Who's there?" he called toward the living room, his voice and hand wavering. "Danny?"

He knew it wasn't Danny, but couldn't bring himself to admit who he thought it might be—who it *had* to be. The front door was bolted shut. The back door always was. It was possible someone had entered the house from his upstairs bedroom—he preferred to keep the window open to allow a cool draft while he slept. But that would require a tall ladder, something he didn't even have on his property.

James rushed through these thoughts, eliminating each as quickly as they entered his mind.

A lamp in the living room provided the only light, a soft glow from his position in the kitchen. His eyes danced across the kitchen, scanning the open space that led to the living room. A tall shadow dashed across the wall, freezing the blood in his veins as his grip tightened on the knife. James debated calling out again, hoping to startle whoever had sneaked into his house, but kept silent for the moment, trying to catch the perpetrator off guard. It was his house, and he had the advantage of knowing its layout with his eyes shut.

James moved closer to the living room, working toward the wall when he could keep his back against it and not worry about an attack from behind. Once he was within a couple of steps, he lunged into the living room, knife jabbing in front of him as he prepared for the intruder to attack.

No one was there.

"What the fuck?" he whispered, adrenaline pulsing from his toes to his fingertips on the knife's handle. The living room remained undisturbed, everything in its proper place. The TV flicked on, and James gasped, jumping backward into the wall and rattling a couple of framed pictures.

The sound of whispering voices filled his head, seeming to ooze from the walls. Their words were inaudible, jumbled together as if hundreds of people were speaking at the same time. "Stop it!" James shouted, covering his left ear with his free hand and cocking his head sideways to bury his other ear in his shoulder without having to drop the knife. "STOP IT!"

He apparently shouted loud enough to cease the whispering, the house falling silent for a moment before a childish giggle bounced around the walls, once again surrounding James as he slunk to the ground, his legs having given out.

The laughter lasted only a few seconds, and James realized he had started crying, salty liquid pooling on the tip of his nose. Fear swallowed him and jaded all of his senses as he continued to scan the living room for the source of the madness.

"Is this a nightmare?" he asked. "Wake me up!"

Another round of laughter showered the room, followed by a young woman's chilling voice. "This isn't a nightmare, Sheriff, but I am!"

James didn't need to hear any more to know who the voice belonged to. There simply weren't any more dots to connect.

"Amelia?" James called out, his mind fighting to process what was unfolding. Suddenly, death seemed the most likely way for this day to end, mere hours after the active town sheriff had left his property. Minutes after Danny Espinoza, who seemed to have all the answers, had vanished into the woods.

Just buy some time. Maybe the kid can pull this off before she can make a move.

He stayed against the wall, figuring out the best the course of action to take to survive at least the next hour. He could remain where he was, and force Amelia to come out and confront him. She was likely trying to lure him somewhere else in the house, but he had no way of knowing how she wanted to play this twisted game. The thought of her having an axe again somehow was a growing concern. He'd be no match with his chef's knife.

I need to get upstairs and get my gun.

His eyes fell on the front door, and he considered making a run for his truck. Only his keys were on the other side of the living room, and he didn't trust it would be as simple as hopping into his truck to drive away. Amelia wouldn't have that. He also didn't know how he would fare driving under the strenuous circumstances. Driving at night was already a challenge for him, adding the sheer panic flowing through his body would surely lead to him crashed into a ditch or wrapped around a tree.

"Sheriff?" Amelia's voice called, no obvious source of where from.

"Get out of my house, you bitch!" James snarled, rising back to his feet with a death grip on the knife. "You think I'm afraid of you? Come out and fight me, you chickenshit!"

Amelia responded with more laughter, her presence seeming to float in the air, encircling James in a hurricane of horror. "Oh, Sheriff, you are such the flattering man. Only one of us is leaving this house tonight. I came here for my jewelry box, and I'm not leaving without it."

James felt his stomach drop at the mention of the box. He suddenly had leverage. Hell, everyone involved had leverage at this point. The box was gone, and that wasn't even a lie he'd have to tell.

"You're too late, Amelia. The box has been taken. They're going to destroy it, and send you back to hell."

James, suddenly calm and confident, took a step off the wall.

"NO!" Amelia screamed, rumbling the house, the glasses in the kitchen cupboards clinging together before everything fell still and silent. A heavy thud came from above, where James's bedroom was, before even heavier footsteps rumbled down the stairs at the opposite end of the living room.

Amelia moved with such speed, James only caught a glimpse of her before she dashed into the kitchen at the other entrance.

Okay, she's down here, let's do this, he thought, inching backward and turning to face the kitchen straight on. They could technically walk in circles all night thanks to the kitchen having two entryways from the living room.

"Amelia?" James called out once again, the knife trembling in his grip. He didn't see an axe when she came down the stairs, and already felt the odds shifting back in his favor.

She didn't respond. Instead, a gunshot blasted from the kitchen, followed by the unmistakable thud of a body hitting the ground, the gun clattering as it slid across the kitchen floor and into James's line of sight.

James stood frozen, mind racing out of control. "She shot herself?" he whispered in disbelief, eyes glued to the gun. He stood there for an entire three minutes, eyes on the gun, ears focused on the silence, trying to hear anything from the kitchen that might suggest Amelia was still alive.

The only thing he heard during that time was the sound of his own breathing. He wanted to call out her name again, but his throat had swelled with tension, forming a boulder that didn't allow him to speak.

James lurked forward, entering the kitchen to find the body of Amelia Doss splayed on the floor, right below the evidence box full of her old belongings. She had come for her jewelry box and shot herself upon realizing it was gone.

Amelia lay facedown, all four limbs spread in different directions, her hair pooling over her face to conceal a ghastly countenance. There was no blood, but James saw the hole in Amelia's head, a never-ending pit of darkness.

I guess serial killers raised from the dead don't bleed, he thought, crouching down to the dead body, hovering over her head for a closer look at the exit wound.

Just as his curiosity had piqued, and he reached out to touch the hole—wanting some sort of confirmation it was all real—the hole morphed shut, a new scalp wriggling across the wound and sealing it shut.

Amelia's hand shot out and grabbed James's ankle, yanking his leg toward her and knocking him on his back. His head hit the kitchen floor, stars lighting up his vision that had temporarily blurred.

Amelia growled as she rose to her knees, the sound no different from a rabid dog ready to pounce. James rolled over and flailed for the gun, but it was too far out of reach. The growling behind him ended just as a sharp pain shot up from his ankle.

"Aw, fuck!" James screamed, sweat dripping from his forehead. He looked down to see Amelia's teeth sinking into his ankle, jerking her head from side to side until a chunk of flesh ripped off. He watched as his flesh dangled from her mouth, and she slurped it in to swallow it whole.

The room spun as he tried to crawl, slipping since his hands couldn't find a grip on the slick floor. Amelia jumped to her feet, grabbed the cast-iron skillet James always left on the stovetop, and promptly swung it, connecting with his skull with a disturbing *thunk!*

Amelia stepped over James and rolled him over, his head cloudy and surely concussed. She dropped to her knees, cradling his torso.

The last thing James Abbott saw in his storied life was the sharp fangs of a monster, just before they clasped around his throat.

27

Getting children to trust and walk away with her had never been difficult in the past for Amelia. Children often left to their own devices would easily go off with her if she presented the opportunity. Getting hold of Charlotte Reynolds proved to be a bit more difficult. The opportunity to snatch the child and run off with her didn't present itself right away. And snatching the child was difficult when Avery was dragging them around town with her while she ran errands. Taking the girl right from under her mother's nose in public also meant traveling through town with a three-year-old, something Amelia would have to regain her physical body for.

Amelia stalked them, waiting for the right time, thinking she'd have to wait until night fell.

Avery's errand run threw a wrench in the plan. She watched from a corner in the shoe store. "Come on, put your old shoes back on so we can buy the new ones and then we'll go back to Grandma's."

"I don't know where my shoes are," Wyatt protested, throwing himself onto one of the store's benches in a melodramatic tantrum that lacked any conviction other than a heavy sigh.

"Come on, Wyatt. Mommy doesn't have all day and Grandma is making bologna sandwiches for lunch. You love those. Check under that other bench. See? Your shoes are right there." Avery turned back to packing the new shoes into their boxes, not bothering to wrap them the same way they'd been when she opened the box.

Charlotte wore a pink flowered shirt and black leggings with pink triangles on them. A fluorescent green tutu was around her waist. On her bare feet, she wore white bunny slippers. "I'm ready, Momma."

Avery turned toward her daughter and let out an amused laugh. "Where did you get those? Take those off and put your own shoes back on." Then she furrowed her brow. "Girl, you have no sense of matching outfits."

Charlotte giggled and removed the bunny slippers, tossing them onto the bench. "Where are my shoes?"

"Look under the bench you're sitting on." Avery shook her head.

Amelia, having had her own children, knew what was next.

When Avery turned to herd Wyatt up to the front counter, Charlotte approached her with snow boots. "Can you help me put these boots on?"

"Honey, you don't need boots. It's dry and warm outside and those will be too hot. Get your own shoes." She pointed at her daughter's shoes, then picked up the snow boots and put them back. Because Charlotte was still dilly-dallying, she grabbed her daughter's shoes from under the bench. "Put your black flats on." She handed them to Charlotte, quickly rethinking the idea, and knelt to help her daughter put the shoes on. "Okay, are we ready?"

Wyatt nodded. "Do we get bologna sandwiches when we get there? Or do we have to wait?"

"Yes, when we get there," Avery said in exasperation, though Amelia guessed she was probably lying in order to make Wyatt more cooperative.

Amelia settled into the wall of the shoe store, only slipping through it every few seconds to see if they'd gone yet. Then she realized it was still early enough that the children might play outside, and that made things easier. The house Tyler Reynolds grew up in had a huge backyard with plenty of nooks and crannies, backing up to the open space that led right into the woods and up the mountain where the mine was. A sly grin made its way onto her lips. She floated out of the shoe shop.

She moved along the roof and down the side of the building, then to the dark crevices of concrete, slipping through the old town like a snake. When she made it to the first major roadway, she paused and looked both ways before crossing. While the cars couldn't hurt her, she didn't like the sensation of trying to move forward while tires went through her and scattered her form, requiring her to come back together again. It made getting to her destination take more time. So she waited until the road was clear and moved across it as quickly as she could. The daylight made her ethereal body more sluggish. She traversed neighborhoods and avoided all of the dogs, who could sense her presence, and finally found herself in more familiar territory. This was a neighborhood she recognized well. She'd spend a lot of time here, back when Tyler was in high school, back when she'd first returned to Ridgeway. When she found Tyler's parents' house, she immediately sought refuge beneath a hedge on the side, scaring off a small rabbit that had been using the hedge for shelter.

The hedge not only provided comforting darkness but

also a good vantage point by which to watch the street. She must have dozed off, because the sound of car doors slamming brought her to, and she peered out from the hedge to see Avery and the children had returned. Now it was a matter of listening and paying attention.

Wyatt was insistent on an *immediate* bologna sandwich, which his grandmother dutifully provided. Charlotte didn't want to eat. She wanted to play outside in the backyard. This was the chance Amelia had been waiting for.

Amelia floated around the house, through the slats on the wooden fence, and into the yard. The elder Reynolds couple didn't have a dog, and that made Amelia's job much easier. She moved past the new, fenced-in pool, to the end of the yard, taking refuge in more bushes that bordered the fence, and waited.

Fifteen minutes later, the children came outside. Wyatt, carrying a yellow truck and a shovel, headed straight to the sandbox. Charlotte, however, skipped and danced her way over to the flowers and began singing "You Are My Sunshine" to them. She didn't appear to know the actual words.

Amelia moved closer to the flower bed, then gave a cursory glance toward the house, only catching Avery looking out for a moment before returning to whatever she was doing. That's when Amelia changed into Alice and whispered, "Charlotte."

Charlotte stopped what she was doing and walked nearer to the bushes, standing on her tiptoes even though that likely wouldn't have helped her see anything better. "Alice?"

"Yes, it's me, but I don't want your brother to see me."

The three-year-old turned to her brother, who was completely immersed in his own playtime without a care for his little sister. He was busy making roads in the sand for his dump truck. Charlotte came around the bush and knelt next to Alice. "What are you playing?"

"Forest," Amelia replied. Children had wild imaginations, that much she knew, and she knew Charlotte would completely accept this without question.

She did. "I want to play, too."

Amelia nodded and handed her a stray stick she found on the ground. "That's your walking stick."

"Where are we walking to?"

Amelia shrugged her shoulders. "We'll go to the mountains and search the fairy mines for magic fairy dust."

Charlotte nodded emphatically. "Okay."

"Charlotte? What are you doing in the bushes?" Avery had half her body leaning out the back door.

She popped out of her spot, still sporting her stick. "I'm going into the mountains to the fairy mines to find fairy dust!"

"Well, that explains that," Avery said before going back inside.

This would not be easy. Avery kept a trained eye on her children, and Amelia would only have a short time to grab the little girl and make off with her. Plus, they had to traverse an open area the length of a soccer field before the woods would hide them.

Avery emerged again and set two glasses of water on a small table just outside the back door. "Here are some drinks if you want them. Grandma and I are going to be watching a show so if you need anything, come in and get us and don't leave the backyard."

"Okay, Mommy," Charlotte hollered from behind the bush.

"Okay," Wyatt echoed, clearly disinterested in anything but his truck.

"Let's go to the fairy mine in the mountains. It's not far," Alice whispered to Charlotte.

Charlotte only nodded and followed, and they crawled

behind the bushes and behind the garden shed. There, a part of the fence was missing, and the opening was just the right size for two small children to escape.

Amelia, in her child-sized body, went through it.

Charlotte paused. "We can't go out there. We'll get in trouble."

"We won't get in trouble. The fairies will bring us back, and no one will even know we went. Plus, we'll come back with fairy dust," Amelia promised. "It will be a fun adventure. We'll only be gone for ten minutes."

She smiled as the child stepped through the fence.

Amelia held out her hand. "Let's go. We'll have to run fast."

Charlotte nodded, took Amelia's hand, and they ran as fast as their small legs could carry them through the field. Amelia kept going. The child almost fell a few times, but Amelia was able to yank her back to her feet and keep going. No worried screams or sounds of pursuit came from behind them. It wasn't until they were safely in the shadows of the woods that Amelia let Charlotte slow down. She turned to the girl, expecting to see tear-stained cheeks and fearful eyes. Instead, she faced a winded, but curious Charlotte.

"Where's the fairy mine?"

Amelia smiled. The little girl had moxie, she'd give her that. "It's just up here." She pointed toward the mine and took Charlotte's hand again as they continued to make their way up the incline of the mountain.

About halfway up, Charlotte stopped. "I need a break, and we forgot the water."

"I can carry you the rest of the way," Amelia offered. "I think the fairy caves have water in them."

"You're not big enough," Charlotte said.

"I can make myself bigger."

Charlotte tipped her head, her eyes widening as if to say, *prove it*.

Amelia morphed into her former self, all grown up.

Tyler's daughter seemed impressed by this. "Wow. How did you do that, Alice?"

"Don't tell anyone, but I'm a fairy." Amelia put her finger to her lips. "Also, when we get to the fairy mines, my friends there call me Amelia."

"Why don't they call you Alice?"

"Alice is only my name when I'm a little girl."

Charlotte took this information in stride and lifted herself from the ground, holding out her arms so Amelia could pick her up.

Amelia hefted the child up into her arms and began moving toward the mine again.

"I thought fairies were tiny. Like Tinkerbell," Charlotte said.

"I can be really big or really small whenever I like." Amelia gave her what she hoped was a pleasant smile. All that mattered was that having Charlotte would bring Tyler to her so she could kill him once and for all. What happened to his daughter after he was dead didn't matter to her.

They arrived at the mine much quicker now that Amelia could move at her own speed. Here in the woods, the shadows were deep and life-giving. Before going into the entrance, Amelia set the girl down and took her hand. "Are you ready to go inside?"

Charlotte eyed the mine entrance warily. "What's that noise in there?"

"Those are my friends. They whisper a lot. You'll get to meet them."

"Okay." Children were so trusting.

With that, Amelia led Charlotte into the mine to meet her friends. They walked through the dark, Charlotte not panicking in the pitch dark, until they reached the first chamber. There, on the far side of the room, a red, eerie glow surfaced from the wall, illuminating the entire room. Amelia looked around. "Where did this light come from?" she asked the shadows.

"Azazoth left it for us," one of them hissed from her left.

Charlotte looked toward the voice. "I'm Charlotte." She held out her hand to the darkness in greeting.

"Charlotte," the shadows chorused.

❧ 28 ❧

Charlotte was asleep and Amelia saw no harm in leaving a few shadows to watch after the child while she and some of her minions left the mine to go down to her grave to prepare for Tyler's arrival. At least, she hoped her nemesis was smart enough to come here without prodding. Ideally, it would have been easier if he came up to the mine. She didn't want to leave any stones unturned, though. The last time, they'd headed straight to the gravesite. This time, she needed to be one step ahead of them.

Wanting to feel the cool evening breeze against her skin, she solidified and stretched her arms out alongside her. It felt strange having a physical body, almost cumbersome in a way. The joints and sinew limited her movement, and the flesh shell confined her breath. She started down the mountain, her posse of shadows at her heels.

Amelia and the shadows arrived at the clearing a few minutes later and looked around. The cemetery, while overgrown, still looked as it did when she'd buried her family all those years ago. Her eyes went to the large tree where she'd faced the noose. She looked away, shoving down the painful memory that threatened to surface and drag her into a blood-thirsty rage. All the same, it reminded her exactly why she was doing this. Randall Nelson. He'd murdered her, most brutally. Tyler Reynolds was Randall's kin. While she'd given up on the idea that Tyler and Randall were the same exact person, she hadn't yet ruled out reincarnation. But even if that wasn't the case, Tyler was payback for what Randall had done to her. That's all she wanted. Revenge. She would do to him what Randall had done to her. There was no more time or energy left for creativity. No, this time she would just slit his throat, throw him into the grave, and be done with it.

"Amelia?" one shadow asked, dragging her from her memories.

"Dig up that grave." She pointed to the grave where her physical body had been unceremoniously dumped all those years ago.

She could feel their eyes on her, their questioning eyes. The shadows knew that was her grave.

"Dig it up," she repeated, her voice hollow.

Her friends went to work, heaping round balls of earth from the ground and chucking the soil to one side. Inch by inch, the hole went deeper. When it was somewhere between four to five feet deep, they stopped, gathering around the grave to look over the edge.

"What's wrong? Why have you stopped?" She sounded more like their supervisor than their trusted bosom friend.

"The bones," they whispered in unison.

Amelia inched toward the grave, almost afraid to look over the edge. But she did it anyway. There, sticking out of the ground, her pale bones gleamed up at her. She turned away. "That's deep enough. Let him lay atop my bones so that we are forever united in death."

"How will we kill him?" one of the shadows pressed.

She was tired. Oh, so tired. "I will kill him, and that will be the end. Finally. I need no interference from you."

The shadow withdrew. They knew to do that when they caught her in a mood.

"I will kill him quickly and throw him into the grave. Then we will bury him," she said, this time her voice decided and curt. The pleasure she'd previously felt when she imagined killing Tyler, the maiming and dismemberment, was all but gone, leaving her numb. It felt strange. Hollow.

"What of the child and Tyler's friend?" another shadow asked.

"You may do with them what you wish. Kill them, let them live. I don't care. I grow weary." Everything felt solemn then. In that moment, Amelia wanted nothing more than a release from this prison of flesh and the bloodlust that often consumed her.

With the grave dug, she turned back toward the mine. "We should return." Then her mind drifted to Azazoth. "Why did Azazoth not die?"

The shadows, who usually whispered amongst themselves and sounded like a thousand buzzing bees, went completely silent.

Amelia stopped walking and turned to them, catching a few ducking out of sight behind trees. There was something they weren't telling her. She glowered at them. "Tell me."

"He wasn't dead, just resting," one of them volunteered.

Amelia snorted and turned back to the trail. It had been nice not having Azazoth around. It took his absence to make her realize she hadn't really missed him.

Behind her, the shadows kept their distance, slinking through the growing darkness, their whispers sounding more like a breeze. She couldn't catch what they were saying, but she didn't care. She had few hours left on this earth and she planned to spend them in quiet contemplation of a peaceful afterlife.

When they returned, the shadows slunk off into the mine, leaving Amelia alone outside. The air grew more frigid, but she didn't feel the cold so much. She tried to remember what cold felt like, but the best she could do was recollect her disdain for it. It was uncomfortable, like starched muslin. No, that wasn't it. What did it feel like? She put her hands to her head and stared straight ahead, trying to remember.

"You won't be able to remember. You're no longer living. You're not quite dead." Azazoth crouched down next to her.

"Oh. It's you." She gave him a sideways glance.

"You'll never feel the cold against your skin or the heat from the sun. You'll never experience the pain of wounded flesh."

"But I remember the pain," Amelia said.

"You remember the fear," Azazoth corrected.

She turned to him then, her eyes boring through him. She wanted to argue with him and scream at him and ask him why he wasn't dead.

"You don't wish to do any of those things. You know I'm right."

A friend, she thought, *would never say such things*.

"Only a friend would say such things." Azazoth remained unfettered by her growing emotional turmoil.

"Why didn't you die?"

"I wasn't dying."

"Then what were you doing, curled up in a ball, drifting out of consciousness? I thought shadows never slept." She narrowed her eyes, thinking there was something sinister about Azazoth.

A sly grin slid over his lips, and he chuckled. "I have been alive for billions of years. I am older than this Earth, child.

Older than the fire and gas that birthed this galaxy. I am chaos. I am one of the elder gods."

"Then why did you lie down in a mine and look like you were dying?" She didn't understand his archaic mutterings. Everyone knew there was only one God. One creator. Azazoth certainly wasn't Him. He was a bastard, surely, but Azazoth was a mere shadow. Just like her, only older.

He knew what she was thinking, and he put on a wry smile. "You'll have to learn the hard way."

Now she glared at him. A real friend would have given her a pep-talk, perhaps helped her reclaim her joy in killing. She should have been excited—no, ecstatic—to kill Tyler Reynolds. To get back at Randall Nelson. To destroy him like he'd destroyed her. "You know nothing."

"As you wish," Azazoth said. Then he stood and retreated into the mine with the rest of the shadows and Charlotte Reynolds.

Amelia ran her hand over her arm. Even touch didn't feel the same. Something odd was happening to her. Her mouth was no longer moist, nor dry. Her skin was neither soft nor rough. Colors were no longer vibrant. Even crimson streams of blood didn't have the same depth that they used to.

She let out a heavy sigh, realizing that even her breath didn't feel the same. Perhaps Azazoth was right. She was changing into something different. Changing from being human and dead to something else. And she didn't like it. It wasn't like she had a choice, though. Grinding her teeth together, she concluded that at some point, she'd have to swallow her pride and ask Azazoth more questions.

Inside her, a spark of hatred for Azazoth grew. She hated that he was right. She hated that he knew far more than he would tell her. And most of all, she hated how he spoke in riddles and was rarely forthright about anything.

Even her hatred, though, had dimmed. It didn't feel the

same as it used to. It was no longer a bright fire raging in her chest. There was no longer the rush of excitement or adrenaline. She's been so busy killing and laying waste to anyone who crossed her, and it had happened so gradually that she'd barely noticed it. Until now.

Azazoth returned. "It's almost time."

She stood up and turned to him. "Will you be coming down to the gravesite to observe?"

"I'll come," he said.

It was completely black by the time one shadow returned to report that Tyler and Danny had arrived and were making their way up to the old family cemetery.

"Draw them up here," Amelia ordered.

The shadows obliged, creating a cacophony of noise by smacking rocks against boulders and banging sticks together. But none of the ruckus appeared to draw Tyler and Danny any closer. Amelia narrowed her eyes and turned to go back inside the cavern, only to trip over Charlotte, who, while groggy, somehow made her way out of the mine on her own.

"Amelia, what's all this noise? I have to go home now." The little girl looked up at the sky. "It's nighttime. My momma is gonna be mad."

"Well, lucky for you it's not your mother who's come to get you. It's your father," Amelia said.

"My daddy? Where?" Her small eyes darted around the clearing, but there was no sign of him anywhere.

"Unfortunately, we'll have to go find him. I'm afraid he and Danny got lost," Amelia said, her voice now cold, barren of any human emotion, if she'd ever had any.

This didn't faze Charlotte. "Uncle Danny!" She took Amelia's hand, pulling back when Amelia yanked it away and glowered at the child.

Rethinking her reaction, she grabbed the child by the

hand and dragged her a few steps toward the direction of the graves.

This time, Charlotte started to cry.

The crying enraged Amelia, and she thought about grabbing the little girl by the throat and crushing her windpipe. Shutting her up for good. But then she heard one of her shadow friends whisper something softly in her ear.

"Possess the child," it hissed.

Could she even do that? Her eyes narrowed. Tyler wouldn't even see her coming. It was brilliant. If the shadow beside her had form, she would have hugged it. Instead, she shifted from her physical form to a soft black mist, looked down at the still sniveling brat beside her. Then she dove down the little girl's throat.

It was nice and dark inside Charlotte Reynolds. Amelia pushed her way through the bones and flesh until her presence filled the child completely. Then she practiced moving a leg, then an arm, then the head. She felt like she was wearing a child-suit. A cackle emerged from her mouth—well, Charlotte's mouth. She even sounded like Tyler's daughter.

How glorious, she thought. Then she opened her eyes, surprised when the child's eyes opened, too. Charlotte, the real Charlotte, was in there, too, but she couldn't move or control anything and all Amelia sensed was pure fear. This made her smile even wider. She took a few steps, her toddler body jerking awkwardly. Knowing she'd have to overcome the poor motor skills of a small child, she became more determined.

Amelia, wearing the Charlotte suit, began making her way down the side of the mountain toward the family cemetery and Tyler's freshly dug grave.

＊ 29 ＊

Tyler's phone rang, and he snatched it up immediately, expecting a call from Danny who had informed him he had the jewelry box, but wanted to first stop by the museum to find any cross-reference that might confirm Amelia Doss had a connection to the box.

It wasn't Danny, but instead a number he didn't recognize. "Hello?"

"Mr. Reynolds, this is Sheriff Lloyd. Are you okay?"

"Yes. What is going on?"

His mind immediately jumped to Danny, thinking he was in some sort of trouble.

"I forgot my hat at James' and went back to get it, and... well, James Abbott is dead," she replied, taking a deep breath. "Do you know anything about this?"

"Dead?!" Tyler gasped. His head spun as he tried to piece together this sudden news. "I . . . no. Well—"

"You and your friend have been working with him on this Amelia Doss stuff, haven't you?" Sheriff Lloyd asked.

"Yes." He had no reason to lie now.

The sheriff lowered her voice. "I need to know what the

hell is going on. Tell me everything. Once the town hears of this, hell will break loose. I need to have an explanation before that happens, or else there will be chaos. Where are you?"

"I'm at Danny's house. He's at the museum. We're trying to send Amelia Doss back to the grave tonight."

"And you're absolutely certain it's her? She would have been the one to do this to Sheriff Abbott?"

"It has to be. She's gotten stronger. We think she's responsible for all the murders that have been happening."

"And no one bothered alerting me? I'm the one who actually *believed* you all those years ago, Tyler. Did you forget that already?"

"Of course not. It's just—we don't entirely understand what we're dealing with. We didn't want to put anyone else in the line of danger who didn't need to be."

"That is literally my job. Look, we don't have time to dwell. I need to work on this crime scene and find something that is at least believable to share with the public. Are you two going to finish this tonight, or do we need to brace for more?"

"It will be done tonight," Tyler said confidently, not having any idea if they were close or not.

"Do whatever you need, and call me if you need help with anything. I mean it."

"Yes, ma'am."

Sheriff Lloyd hung up without another word. Tyler grabbed his keys, raced to his car, and sped away from Danny's house to meet him at the museum. He dialed him while he drove, but didn't get an answer. Driving at lightning speed, it only took him five minutes to arrive, speeding toward the door on feet that moved faster than his mind could comprehend.

He barged into the museum and immediately called out

Danny's name. Tyler scanned the lobby, the building deserted since it was closed to the public. Mannequins and portraits stared at him from across the main floor's display.

Danny appeared down the hallway, the jewelry box clenched in his grip. "Ty? What are you doing here?"

"Dan! Sheriff Abbott is dead. She killed him. We need to move now!"

They ran toward each other, Danny's face contorted in terror. "I was just at this house. There was nothing there. I don't understand."

"We don't have time to understand—we need to put Amelia back in the grave right now."

Tyler's phone rang again. "What is it now?!"

This time the call was from his wife, and his heart sunk. He didn't even have time to speak upon answering, Avery promptly spitting out words.

"Ty, Charlotte is missing. We've been searching for her for the last hour and have no idea where she went. She was talking about voices in the walls earlier. I think Amelia has her."

Tyler didn't know how to respond, his jaw dropping open as his mind felt like a pinball machine.

"Tyler, did you hear me?!" Avery asked, her voice quivering.

"Yes, don't panic. I'm on it."

Tyler hung up without a clue what he was to do next, feeling sick that he had just left his panicking wife clueless what would happen with their missing daughter. Danny watched the phone conversation and waited with arms crossed and a bouncing leg.

"She has Charlotte," Tyler said, the words feeling dirty and shameful as they left his lips. *How could I have let it come to this point? It was only a matter of time.*

"Get in my car," Danny said. "Let's go."

He pushed by Tyler and headed for the exit, not turning off the lights or worrying about closing anything inside. He locked the door once they were outside, and that was all he needed to do in the moment.

Tyler followed, his legs turning into Jell-O with each step, an overwhelming sense of dread devouring him as his life slipped from his own control.

"Hurry!" Danny shouted over his shoulder, already opening his car door and firing up the engine.

The moment Tyler sat down, Danny sped off, burning rubber as they blazed out of the museum's parking lot. The museum was at the eastern end of Main Street, and Danny drove west. The late hour afforded them little traffic, Danny even slowing at red lights, but continuing through them once he saw no oncoming traffic.

Tyler assumed they were going to his parents' house to meet with Avery and figure out what to do next, but he passed that turn. After they passed the police station, Tyler asked, "Where are we going?"

"To Amelia's grave," Danny replied flatly, his eyes focused like lasers on the road ahead.

"What?! Dan, I want this as much as you, but we don't have time. Charlotte is missing—we have to go get her!"

"I need you to trust me. We have everything we need. Charlotte is going to be just fine." Danny patted the jewelry box that he had put on the middle console between them. "I'm confident this is what we need to destroy. The ritual will work this time."

"What about Charlotte?"

"Nothing will happen to her—I promise. She's being used as a pawn. Charlotte is being used to lure you, but we're going to ignore Amelia's games and send her back to the grave."

"How can you be so sure?" Tyler had an impossible time believing Amelia Doss wouldn't harm his daughter while having her in her clutches.

"Because I've learned too much. Amelia doesn't know how to adapt. She's become too used to having all control and power throughout her life. She assumes people will bow to her demands. This is your mother's situation all over again, but this time we know what to expect. Amelia can stay wherever she is with Charlotte. If Charlotte is harmed, she knows you'll be too out of control to kill. She wants you scared and willing to do whatever she asks."

"So we're just going to ignore her and trust the universe nothing happens to Charlotte?"

"We're beyond trusting. I have faith in myself that this is going to work. It would have worked last time, but we had the wrong object. Everything Sheriff Abbott said about the jewelry box suggests that it's what we need. I flipped through some old pictures I kept at the museum. I saw this box in a photo of Amelia brushing her hair in front of her vanity. This is *it*."

They had left town behind, the darkness of the mountains swallowing their surroundings, leaving them unable to see anything outside of the coverage from the headlights on the road ahead. Danny navigated through the twists and turns of the road, slowing as they reached the abandoned Myers property.

All Tyler could think about during the hectic drive was the lives lost. The lives she had first taken as a mortal human being over a century ago. And of course the murders she had committed since her return from the grave fifteen years earlier, leading up to today. He even felt fortunate. With all the death surrounding him, inching closer as Amelia fought to kill him, only Bryson Day had been someone truly within his inner circle of friends and family. His parents were okay. His wife and kids were still alive, even if Amelia had Charlotte. And he had Danny, the loyal friend who never wavered in the face of terror. His friend who took full responsibility for unleashing Amelia Doss back upon the world. Without Danny's dedication to righting his wrong, Tyler figured everyone he loved would be dead by now, himself included.

His heart ached for James Abbott. How cruel could the world be to take life from a man who had done so much good for his community? A man who had just started a new chapter in his life, but got sucked back into his inner drive to do further good and keep people safe? They already enshrined Mr. Abbott at the town's museum, and his tragic death would only add to his legacy. Tyler could only hope the ex-sheriff would be Amelia's final victim.

Danny pulled into the driveway of the abandoned home and killed the engine and headlights, leaving them in pure blackness while crickets chirped outside, playing their symphony to set the stage for Danny's last stand.

While they didn't know for sure where Amelia had taken Charlotte, Tyler assumed it was the house standing in front of him, or the mine further up the mountain. A climb to the mine at this late hour would prove difficult and exhausting, exactly what Amelia would want him to struggle through before meeting her. The house appeared undisturbed, so he ruled that out once confirming no lights or candles had been illuminated inside.

The hardest part for Tyler would be maintaining the discipline to not wander up the mountain to the mine. Standing around Amelia's grave while his daughter was hundreds of yards away, while Danny chanted to the gods, would be near impossible. Faith in Danny could only comfort him to a certain point, and unless he saw actual activity confirming the ritual was working, he'd have no choice but to track down his daughter and save her.

"Keep quiet," Danny said, grabbing a flashlight as he opened his door and stepped outside.

Tyler followed suit, picking up his own flashlight, trailing behind Danny as they made their way around the Myers house, toward the back. Tyler peered through every window for further confirmation no one was inside.

Danny finally pulled out his cell phone and used its flashlight to illuminate the path ahead, weaving through trees and shrubs on their way to the gravesite.

Tyler bumped into him when he came to a sudden stop, but Danny didn't say anything, keeping his stare ahead. "What the hell?"

Tyler followed the beam of light to an open hole in ground, big enough to bury a body, right below the headstone of Amelia Doss.

"Her grave is already dug out," Danny whispered to himself.

"I don't understand."

"Me neither. Why would her grave be dug out? That doesn't even need to be done for the ritual to work."

"Coincidence?" Tyler asked. "All these murders going on around town, maybe some kids thought they'd come look to make sure Amelia's body is where it's supposed to be."

"Maybe *she* did it. Maybe she knows what we're up to and is trying to throw us off. It doesn't matter, though—I'm still doing the ritual, and this won't influence it."

Tyler sensed doubt in Danny's voice, but knew his friend would never admit to it. If someone had been to the grave, was it possible they had also ventured up to the mine? How much did other people know about Amelia Doss? This new surprise planted doubt for Tyler, and he had no problem accepting it. Literally standing between a pending ritual and his kidnapped daughter, he felt the world pressing down, forcing a split-second decision in a moment that required caution and calculation.

Danny made it all easier as he turned off his flashlight and draped them in darkness. "It's time, Tyler. Let's finish this."

$$\maltese \quad 30 \quad \maltese$$

"You realize that I'll let her kill me before I let anything happen to Charlotte." Tyler paused and glanced from the dark outline of the open grave to Danny, and back again. "If I don't make it tonight, I need you to make sure you get Charlotte back to Avery safely."

The weight of crushing responsibility increased, and Danny nodded. "You know that if anything happens to you, I'll throw myself in front of any danger to make sure she's safe." What else could he say? After all, if it hadn't been for his screwing around when they were back in high school, none of this would be happening now. Living with that guilt all these years had been the hardest for Danny. He usually tried to ignore it by consoling himself with the idea that maybe it wasn't just him. Maybe it was the collective belief of all of them that brought her back in the beginning. At some point, however, he knew he would have to face the fact that he was the one who uttered that stupid incantation. He could hear it echoing in his mind, even now. Sometimes he heard it in his dreams.

. . .

"OH, AMELIA. OH, AMELIA.
For they punished her with death,
yet her spirit never freed.
May her soul rise from the ashes,
but never let her be.
We welcome her to roam the ground she used to walk.
Let her never harm a soul, as long as we all talk."

"I KNOW YOU WILL," TYLER SAID, PULLING DANNY OUT OF the chant playing in his mind.

"Maybe that's it," Danny mumbled.

"Maybe what's it?" Tyler stiffened, and the tension in the air thickened.

"That stupid incantation. I sever the connection to the box and change the original incantation." A wave of fear mingled with excitement washed over him and a chill slipped into his bones.

But Tyler didn't seem to be listening. "We know she wasn't connected to me or the axe, but what if she's not connected to the box, either?"

Danny turned toward Tyler in the dark. "That's what I mean. I'm going to sever any ties with the box, destroy it, and then I'm going to reverse the original incantation." He patted his jacket and felt his notebook and pen. "I just have to rework it. Give me a light."

While Danny shoved his hand into his inner jacket pocket and pulled out the pen and notepad, Tyler lifted his flashlight and clicked it on, aiming it at the notepad in Danny's hand.

"I just need a minute," Danny said, knowing that Tyler would have a hard time sitting still while his youngest child was in the clutches of a demonic serial killer.

Strangely, however, Tyler stood quietly, not moving a

muscle, his eyes focused on the darkness beyond the grave-yard and what lay up the hill.

"Ty, you okay?"

Tyler nodded. "I just need a few minutes, too."

Danny looked back down at his notebook and scribbled the incantation down. He began writing:

Amelia, Amelia - we punish you with death!
Your spirit never freed.
Your soul shall never rise from the ashes.
We will leave you be.
You are not welcome to roam the ground that you used to walk.
We commit you to the grave, and of you we'll never talk.

He stared at the words for a moment, entranced by their power, not realizing Tyler had finally regained his composure and was now watching Danny with great interest. "What?"

Danny shook off the daze he felt from what he'd just written. "Nothing. I think I have it."

Before he could say anything else, Tyler snatched the notebook from his hand and adjusted the flashlight onto the page. He read the words, slowly nodding as he got to the end. "It will have to do. I'll deal with Amelia and get Charlotte. I need you to focus on that box and your anti-summoning." He handed the notebook back to Danny.

Normally, Danny might have laughed at a term like *anti-summoning*, but tonight wasn't that kind of night. He felt his jacket to make sure he had the diesel fuel, matches, lighter, paper, holy water, and his notebook. "Okay, *now* let's do this."

Tyler nodded, but then paused. "Danny—whatever happens—don't stop."

"But what if…"

"No. Keep going. Once you're done with the ritual stuff… then help me, okay?" Even in the dark, Danny could see the resolve in Tyler's eyes.

He nodded. "Okay." He also knew that if Tyler was overpowered, he would do whatever it took, and if history had taught them anything, it was that life and death were unpredictable. There was always that wild card no one accounted for, and if the ritual went smoothly as planned and they walked away with Tyler's daughter, it would be a miracle.

Danny clicked on his flashlight again and aimed the beam of light onto Amelia Doss' now open grave. He went ahead, leaving Tyler behind, and stepped up to the deep hole, training his light into it. He gasped. In the bottom of the hole lay human remains and what was left of a rope. With Amelia's grave having been disturbed multiple times, and the bones not having been there fifteen years ago, Danny was confused, but he didn't have time to reason it out. All he knew was he had to work fast.

Three loud *clacks*, like rock hitting rock, rang out at them from somewhere further up the mountain. Then the whispering started, and within a minute, it was all around them.

"Concentrate, Dan," Tyler told him. Then he screamed into the night, "Charlotte!"

Danny set the box at the foot of the grave. He closed his eyes, imagining the tether from it to Amelia Doss. Unlike the ritual with the axe, this time something clicked.

"Hello, Daddy." Charlotte's voice broke through the whispers.

Danny heard Tyler gasp and then mutter, "Unholy Christ."

His eyes shot open, breaking his link with the box. There, across the clearing, he saw Charlotte standing by herself, but there was something wrong with her. When she walked, her body jerked unnaturally and her eyes had a silver glow to them.

"What have you done to my baby?" Tyler's voice broke.

The child's skin looked normal enough. Pink and vibrant. Blood flowed through her veins. But it was almost like Charlotte was... possessed.

Charlotte spotted the box and her expression changed from creepy doll smile to pissed-off maniacal grin. "Why do you have my box?"

Because the box is the link, Danny's mind screamed. But he couldn't leave Charlotte in that state.

"Danny?" Tyler whispered from his left.

"Amelia possessed your daughter."

Sheer panic entered Tyler's voice. "Get her out."

"The box."

"Shit. What was that exorcism thing?" Tyler's eyes, wide with horror, pleaded with Danny.

As if he, himself, were possessed, Danny picked up the box and put it inside his jacket, then pulled out the holy water and began reciting the exorcism Lavinia had given him. If Amelia wanted the box, she was going to have to kill him to get it.

The Latin flew from his lips with conviction, and he started toward Amelia in little Charlotte's body. He shook some holy water at her, hitting the child right in the face with it.

A blood-curdling shriek came from Charlotte.

Danny repeated the incantation, watching with sheer trepidation as a shadowy figure separated itself from Charlotte's small body and solidified right before their eyes. Amelia could shift from the physical to the spirit world so fluidly.

The whispers around them grew louder, and the shadows began stepping out from behind the trees and underbrush, solidifying into semi-opaque human forms. They were surrounded.

He felt a hand on his shoulder, and his heart almost stopped until he realized it was Tyler's. "You deal with the box. Go."

Danny did as he was told. He threw down the box, doused it with diesel, lit a piece of paper, then held it to the fuel-soaked box. It took longer for the diesel to light, but it burned hotter and more completely. Finally, he did the visualization exercise. The tether from the box leading to Amelia, and the tether snapping as the flames consumed the box.

There was a small crack and an explosion, and Danny found himself thrown backward onto the ground, his ass stinging from the fall. In front of him, the flames devoured the box.

He turned to find Amelia holding Charlotte, her eyes in a panic trained on the flaming box. Tyler closed in on her. Just as he reached out to grab Charlotte, Amelia threw the three-year-old into the grave, a sinister grimace on her face.

She stood between Tyler and the open grave, where the cries and whimpers of Charlotte lifted into the cold night air. "Now I've got you." Amelia said. She held his arm up in the air and her hand turned into a long hunting knife.

"Jesus Christ," Danny muttered. Then his eyes went to the hole. It wasn't that deep. If he could just grab Charlotte.

Amelia lunged forward, bringing her blade down right on Tyler's forearm. Tyler pulled back, one hand moving to protect the wounded flesh. She advanced again, and Tyler retreated, leading her away from the open grave to the other side of the clearing.

Danny took his chance and jumped into the hole, careful not to land on Charlotte. With eyes squeezed shut, Charlotte curled into a ball, whimpering and shaking. He leaned down.

"Charlotte, it's Uncle Danny. Open your eyes. Tell me where you're hurt."

She opened her eyes and began crying. "All over."

He picked her up, feeling for broken bones and finding nothing out of place. It appeared she was whole and intact and bruised and more frightened than anything. It took some doing, but he lifted her up and out of the grave. Then he pulled himself out. He picked her up, realizing he wouldn't have time to grab his notebook. So far, it appeared Tyler was holding his own, though Danny noticed a fresh wound on Tyler's thigh that left him limping.

"You're going into that grave," Amelia spat at him.

Danny visualized the grave being a vacuum, sucking Amelia back into it. "Amelia, Amelia – we punish you with death! Your spirit never freed. Your soul shall never rise from the ashes. We will leave you be. You are not welcome to roam the ground that you used to walk. We commit you to the grave, and of you we'll never talk!"

Charlotte buried her head in Danny's shoulder, clutching onto him for dear life, and he put a protective arm around her.

An icy blast of wind ran through the clearing, knocking Amelia off of her feet. She fell to the ground, clutching it with her fingernails as an unseen force dragged her toward her grave. On the far side of the clearing a grotesque humanoid figure emerged with red eyes and razor sharp, gleaming white teeth.

"It's time to go, Amelia," the thing said in a scratchy voice.

"It's Azzie!" Charlotte clutched Danny for all she was worth.

"Azazoth! Take my hand!" Amelia reached out.

The thing gave her a sinister smile and reached out with a clawed hand.

Tyler skittered the long way round the clearing until he was at Danny's side. "What the hell *is* that?"

Danny shook his head, at a loss for words. Whatever it was, it appeared to be helping Amelia Doss.

"Throw an incantation at it," Tyler commanded.

But Danny couldn't speak. Something froze him to the ground, as if some dark force held him in place and paralyzed his vocal cords.

Amelia took the thing's hand and stood.

"It's time to go," it repeated. "There is nothing keeping you here."

Amelia's face fell, and her lips contorted into a scowl. Her physical body shimmered and faded into its shadowed form. "I'm not finished."

"You *are* finished with this world."

She pulled back, but the creature gripped her. Even when she tried to vanish, she couldn't get away.

"Stop fighting," it said.

As strange as it seemed, Amelia did, her eyes widening with terror. Finally, she asked, "Where are we going?"

"To a place where there is no rest, Amelia Doss. No rest." Then, at Azazoth's command, both he and Amelia Doss vanished into a mist and as gentle as a breeze, slipped into the grave, the dirt around the open grave closing in on the hole as if they were watching the grave being dug in reverse. When it finished, the grave looked almost untouched.

The surrounding whispers diminished until finally there was nothing except silence and the sounds of crickets.

Charlotte stirred in Danny's arms, turning toward Tyler. "Daddy!"

A strange laugh emerged from Tyler. "Charlotte!" He took his daughter from Danny, holding her close. Tears streamed down his face, and he breathed a sigh of relief. "Danny?"

Danny nodded, then bent down and took up his flashlight, lighting up the grave and the ashes left from the box. He used his left hand to fill in the hole, covering the ashes of the box completely. Then he stood up, his insides still jumping, and his eyes met Tyler's. "Is it really over?"

Tyler took him by the elbow with his free hand. "Let's get the hell out of here."

He nodded again and followed. Something about the air felt lighter and by the time they'd reached the car, Danny was certain that was the last they'd ever see of Amelia Doss.

❧

THANK YOU FOR READING! IF YOU ENJOYED THIS SERIES, please leave a review. You can find more books by Andre Gonzalez and Audrey Brice on the following pages.

WANT MORE AMELIA DOSS?
Salvation (#3)
Nightfall (#2)
Resurrection (#1)

Andre Gonzalez

Andre Gonzalez is the international bestselling author of the Wealth of Time Series. He writes thriller and horror books after spending many years reading and studying the works of Stephen King and Dean Koontz. Keeping readers up late and their hearts pumping a bit faster than normal is his ultimate goal when cracking open one of his books.

When he's not writing, you can find Andre buried underneath a long to-do list and/or his three hyper children. He and his wife are raising their family in their hometown of Denver, CO.

https://andregonzalez.net/

Audrey Brice

Audrey Brice writes supernatural thrillers, mysteries, urban fantasy, and horror stories filled with spirits, demons, supernatural creatures, and occult practitioners. Her love for storytelling and all things supernatural and paranormal began at an early age. As S. Connolly she writes books about witchcraft and demonology. She writes paranormal romance and steamy romance as Anne O'Connell, and she writes PG13 epic fantasy and tame romance as S. J. Reisner. An award-winning author, she lives along the front range of the Rocky Mountains with her husband and three spoiled house cats.

http://sjreisner.com/

<u>Followed Home (#1)</u>

A Poisoned Mind (Short Story)

Standalone books:

Snowball: A Christmas Horror Story

By Audrey Brice:

OTS Series: (Urban Fantasy) Outer Darkness, Into Darkness, Rising Darkness, Ascending Darkness, Illuminated Darkness, Within Darkness.

Thirteen Covens: Darkness - the OTS - Thirteen Covens crossover novel.

Wicked Ways Series: (Cozy Mystery) Woefully Wicked, Something Wicked, Thoroughly Wicked, Bloody Wicked, Hauntingly Wicked. **Coming soon**: Deliciously Wicked, Lawfully Wicked, Beautifully Wicked, Technically Wicked.

Thirteen Covens Bloodlines Part One (Urban Fantasy/Supernatural Horror): (Or you can get the stories as individual ebooks or audio books in the Fourteen Tales of Thirteen Covens series).   Includes: A Rising Damp, Temple Apophis, Lucifer's Haven, Shadow Marbas, The Watch, Ba'al Collective, and Order of Eurynome.

Thirteen Covens Bloodlines Part Two (Urban Fantasy/Supernatural Horror): (Right now you can get the stories as individual ebooks in the Fourteen Tales of Thirteen Covens series). Blackrose Coven, Temple Dagon, Cult of Lucifuge. FORTHCOMING: Temple of the Magi, Ashtaroth Briarwood, Circle of the Black Moon, and Tiamat Leviathan.

Thirteen Covens Academy (Urban Fantasy/PNR RH): Coven Born, Coven Society, Coven Cursed

Amelia Doss Series:

Salvation (#3)

Nightfall (#2)

Resurrection (#1)

Stygian: Disciples (Horror/Thriller)- My collection of horror short fiction.

Stand Alone Novels: Dark Prince